SOLDIER'S GAME

SOLDIER'S GAME

JAMES KILLGORE

Kelpies is an imprint of Floris Books
First published in 2011 by Floris Books

The publisher acknowledges subsidy from
Creative Scotland towards the publication
of this volume.

British Library CIP data available
ISBN 978-086315-838-4
Printed in Great Britain
by CPI Cox & Wyman, Reading

FOR EMILY AND MAX

1. TWO LEFT FEET

The referee blew the final whistle. It was another humiliating defeat for Bruntsfield Primary. Ross joined the line-up to shake hands with the opposing P7 boys from South Morningside. Each player muttered the obligatory "good game" but everyone knew it had been nothing but a joke. Ross couldn't bear to look in their eyes.

Barry the coach called them into a post-match huddle.

"Okay guys. Good effort," he said.

"Five-nil?" whined Carl Nelson.

"Yes... well," Barry replied. "Only one goal in the second half."

"Because we switched keepers," said Carl.

Ross looked up at Ying whose face burned red. It wasn't just his fault for letting in those goals. South Morningside had run circles around them all.

"Just need to work a bit more on basic skills," said Barry.

"Like touching the ball," muttered Carl.

"Why don't you give it a rest!" Ross snapped.

"Yes. That's not helpful," Barry added quietly.

Barry never raised his voice – unlike the other coaches at Bruntsfield. Even Miss Frew shouted more at the P6 girls. He was always calm, always upbeat. Nothing ever seemed to dampen his enthusiasm. It had been that way from the very first Saturday morning practice session back in P2 – all of them chasing a ball around the pitch like a flock of pigeons. Somehow, barely, he had always managed to keep the team in order and even to win a few matches. Lately though there had been some talk about Barry's methods among the other parents. This was the fourth straight defeat that season.

His dress sense didn't help much either. Most coaches wore tracksuits but Barry always turned up for training in a baggy wool jacket and trousers with a brown fedora hat. On match days he wore old silk ties and carried the club kit in a battered leather suitcase.

"The guy has never been a winner," Ross had overheard Bob Nelson say that morning. Bob was Carl's dad and he turned up every Saturday morning to holler from the sidelines.

"Pass the ball!"

"Mark up!"

"Tackle!"

"For God's sake – it's football, not ballet class!"

Never once did he offer to help Barry with the coaching. Bob was an executive at Standard Life and far too busy. But that didn't stop him being a critic.

Earlier that morning in the first half Ying had managed to catch a high ball just in front of the goal. He spun quickly and floated it back over the pitch towards Ross at left midfield.

"Down the wing, down the wing," Bob bellowed.

Ross took the pass off his right heel and drove the ball hard down the line, racing a defender in pursuit. What happened then was unclear. Somehow his feet just seemed to tangle underneath, and the next thing Ross knew he was sliding face first across the muddy pitch. His chin came to rest just at the feet of Bob Nelson and a couple of the other dads.

"Is he a left footer?" one asked.

"Yeah," Bob replied. "Both of them."

Ross could still hear the laughter in his head as he walked out of Harrison Park and over the Union Canal. It wasn't the first time that season he'd tripped on thin air. He was the tallest and fastest on the team but sometimes his legs just seemed to go each their own way. Just thinking about it made his ears burn with shame.

Ross turned the corner and headed up Polwarth Terrace towards his grandmother's house. He always went to Pat's after football on Saturday mornings, as there was no one around to look after him at his own house. Mr Anderson left early for his office at the university for some "peace and quiet without any students around". Mrs Anderson drove Ross's younger sister Rachel to a dance studio across town in Portobello. Only his teenage sister Kath would be in the house and she slept until noon.

Now that Ross was nearly twelve he could have let himself into the house. But going to Pat's had become routine and he enjoyed visiting her. Sometimes it seemed she was the only one in the family who really listened to him.

Pat lived in an old stone semi that backed onto the

canal. You could stand at her kitchen window and watch the long narrow boats sail past the bottom of the garden.

The front door into the porch was open and Ross poked his head inside and shouted, "It's me!"

"In the kitchen," Pat called in reply. "Milk's on the boil."

Every Saturday Pat had hot chocolate waiting for him – the best Ross had ever tasted. She bought the powder from a special shop in Bruntsfield. It came all the way from Bolivia and was eighty per cent real cocoa, and the mug was always piping hot and topped with miniature marshmallows floating in a half-melted froth.

Ross sat on the front step and pulled off his muddy boots and socks, along with his shin guards. The cool tiles of the porch floor felt nice under his bare feet. He padded down the hall to the kitchen.

Pat stood at the stove pouring out hot milk from a saucepan – a tall thin lady dressed in baggy dungarees and an old paint-spattered Icelandic jumper. She wore her white hair cut short like a boy's and her eyes were blue as a winter sky. In her later years she'd taken up painting and sculpture and sometimes had exhibitions in a gallery down on Dundas Street.

Pat carried the two steaming mugs over to the kitchen table.

"So how did the match go?"

"Disaster," Ross replied.

"What was the score?" she asked.

"You don't want to know," he said. "Liam, our sweeper, was off sick today and nobody played well."

Ross then told her about the trip-up and Bob Nelson's "two left feet" comment.

"Forget it," said Pat. "That's just a cheap shot from someone who should know better."

"But I am clumsy," he muttered.

Pat cocked an eyebrow.

"Nonsense. You're just growing. It's only a matter of finding your feet."

Ross slumped in his chair.

"But you're my grandmother. They pay you to say that."

She gave him a sudden sharp look.

"Have I ever lied to you about anything?"

Ross shook his head.

It was true. Pat never spared his feelings. Should Ross draw a picture that she didn't like she'd say so and tell him why. Or if he fumbled through a tune on the piano she'd say "needs more practice". Not like other adults who'd gush over any old rubbish.

Pat stood up from the table.

"Finish that mug. There's something I want to show you."

"Now?" Ross replied.

"Yes. Come on. Drink up," she ordered.

"What is it?" Ross asked.

"That'd be telling," she replied. "But I hope you have a head for heights."

Pat rooted through a kitchen drawer for a key. Ross followed her out the back to the garage where she opened a padlock on the door. Along one wall of the junk-filled space hung a long wooden stepladder. Together they lifted it off the metal hooks and carried it back through the kitchen and up the stairway. Pat then pointed to the ceiling above the upper landing. High overhead was a small white wooden hatch.

"Not a word about this to your father," she said. "Maybe you should hold the ladder for me first."

Together they positioned the stepladder under the hatch and Pat climbed slowly up the rungs to the ceiling. She reached up and slid the hatch aside. With effort she managed to pull herself up into the opening. A light appeared first and then Pat's head.

"Your turn," she said. "But slow and careful."

Ross clambered up the rungs without looking down. Pat reached from the opening to give him a hand up. Climbing off the top step and up into the broad ceiling gave Ross a dizzy feeling and he realised it wouldn't be so easy getting back down.

The attic ran the length of the house – a dim, dusty space with a rough ply-board floor nailed over the joists. A single bare light bulb hung just above the hatch casting a dull glow over stacks of cardboard boxes, clothes racks, a dressing mirror half covered by a sheet, an antique set of golf clubs, an old mahogany gramophone. Dead wasps littered every surface and cobwebs billowed in the draft.

Pat had a look around.

"Do you know, I don't think I've been up here once since your grandfather died."

Ross picked up a heavy wooden tennis racket out of an old umbrella stand.

"Where did all this stuff come from?" he asked.

"Oh, it's been accumulating for years – my family, John's family," she replied. "Plenty of hidden treasure up here."

"Treasure?" Ross exclaimed.

"Don't get your hopes up," said Pat. "No gold or jewels – nothing as common as that."

A faint light shone from a stone vent at the far end of the attic. Pat headed towards it, pushing aside the cobwebs.

"Back here if memory serves," she said.

Ross followed, ducking his head to avoid the roof beams. Tucked in a corner against a stone chimney stood a set of rusted metal shelves stuffed with ancient box files and old magazines bound in twine. On the bottom shelf sat a larger object covered with a dustsheet.

Ross peered over her shoulder as Pat reached down to pull away the sheet. Beneath it was a wooden chest with a dull brass catch.

"I thought you were kidding about treasure," said Ross. "What's in there?"

Pat smiled and slid the box off the shelf onto the floor.

"Why don't we take it down to the kitchen for a better look?"

2. AN UNLIKELY TREASURE

Getting the box down from the attic proved tricky. It wasn't so much heavy as awkward in shape. Ross lowered himself first through the ceiling hatch, feeling for the top of the ladder with his foot.

"Good. Now get your balance," said Pat.

He climbed down a couple of rungs and steadied himself before reaching back up for the box. But the ladder began to wobble.

"Is this a good idea?" he asked.

Pat frowned.

"Maybe not."

She pulled the box back into the attic.

"Go on down," she said. "We'll try something else."

Ross climbed to the bottom. He could hear thumps and bumps as Pat rummaged above. After a while she called down, "Move the ladder."

"What?"

"Move it aside."

Ross did as he was told and a minute later the box appeared again in the hatchway bound in a rope sling that Pat had improvised from some washing line. It spun slowly down from the ceiling into Ross's arms.

"Got it!" he shouted.

"Excellent," she called from above. "Now, if someone could just lower me."

Ross pushed the ladder back into place and held it steady as Pat eased herself through the hatch and climbed slowly down to the landing.

"Not a broken bone between us," she puffed.

Ross carried the box downstairs to the kitchen and laid it on the breakfast table. Here in the bright sunlight he could see it was neatly crafted in pine, the wood stained dark maroon under a heavy coat of varnish. Just below the brass catch were the initials HM, hand-painted in gold with elaborate intertwining script.

Ross was desperate to open the box but Pat seemed oddly hesitant. She ran her hand lightly over the lid.

After a few moments Ross looked up and found that she was crying.

"What's the matter?" he asked.

"Nothing. Just me being silly."

She pulled a tissue from the sleeve of her jumper.

"Do you know who owned this box?"

Ross pointed to the initials. "HM?"

Pat smiled and shook her head.

"It belonged to my father, Jack Jordan. He made it himself when he was fifteen years old."

"Your father made this?" asked Ross.

"Yes – in the craft workshop at Boroughmuir High School," Pat replied. "Have a look."

She turned the box around and pointed to an inscription carved neatly in the lower back corner: JJ 1911

Pat brushed her fingers over the marks and then turned the front of the box back towards Ross.

"Go on then. Open it," she said.

Ross reached out to the catch and tried to imagine what he might find inside. Not gold but maybe some valuable family heirloom like on Antiques Roadshow – a collection of old coins or an ivory chess set or letters by somebody famous.

He flicked the small brass hook free of its loop and

lifted the lid. Inside the box, nestled among crumpled yellow newspapers, lay a pair of leather football boots. Pat smiled at the look of disappointment on his face.

"Not what you expected?"

"Not exactly," Ross muttered.

"Well some things are worth more than they look," she said.

"But it's just a pair of old boots," he replied.

Pat sighed.

"Do you know that the year Jack Jordan made this box he played centre forward for both his school and Edinburgh's top boys' football club. But his one ambition then was to someday take to the pitch at Tynecastle for Heart of Midlothian – HM. Three years later that's just what he did."

Ross was dumbstruck.

"Your father played for Hearts?"

"Before the Great War broke out," she replied. "Only for one season..."

But Ross was too excited to listen.

"I remember you told me that he liked football but you never said he played professionally!"

Pat had once shown Ross a black and white portrait of her father. It was on the mantelpiece in her front room. A thin old man dressed in a grey three-piece suit and tie sat in a leather armchair, his walking stick clasped between his knees.

"That's your great-grandfather," she'd said, giving it to Ross to hold as she dusted. "He was just as Hearts mad as you: a club member at Tynecastle for over thirty years. He rarely missed a game."

Ross remembered the face in the picture – pale and gaunt. Pat said that he had died a long time ago. Ross couldn't believe it had never occurred to her to mention that her father had played for his favourite team. He had a million questions.

"Were these his boots at Hearts? What position did he play? Was he a defender, midfielder or a striker? Did he score any goals?"

Pat smiled.

"Let's see what else we can find."

She took out the boots and laid them gently on the table. Underneath the newspaper was a layer of tissue covering a neatly folded strip along with white shorts and thick wool socks. Pat carefully lifted the jersey and held it up to the light – bright maroon with a white collar.

Beneath the clothes was an A4 envelope as well as a small cardboard jewellery box. Pat took out the envelope and spread the contents onto the table. Among the heap of faded football programmes and newspaper clippings was a photograph of a young Jack Jordan dressed in the same kit that now lay on the table before them – a thin but fit young man gazing into the camera with a cheeky, lopsided grin.

Pat held out the photograph and stared across the table at Ross.

"I can definitely see a resemblance," she said.

"Let me look."

Gazing down at the old print Ross could indeed see himself reflected in Jack's face: around the eyes, in the angle of his cheek. It was a little spooky. He handed the photo back to Pat and reached for the jewellery box.

"What's in here?"

Ross opened the lid. Inside, wrapped in cotton wool, was something curious – a small silver badge. It had a circular border and was centred with a crown and interlocking initials in elaborate script. A motto around the outside read: "For King and Empire – Services Rendered".

"What's this doing in a box of football kit?" Ross asked.

"Odd, isn't it," Pat replied. "My father used to

keep it in his top dresser drawer but he must have packed it in the box before he died."

Just then Ross heard the toot of a car horn out in front of the house.

"That's your mother now. Let's get these things back in the box."

"Please. Just a couple minutes more," said Ross.

"No. I don't want to keep her waiting."

Pat packed everything away and Ross gathered his kit. She followed him with the box out into the front hall. Just as he turned to the door she said, "Wait. I want you to have this."

"Me?" said Ross. "But why?"

"Because I want you to keep it safe," she replied.

"Safe? I don't understand."

Pat sighed.

"Safe because I won't be around forever to look after it."

Ross felt a flash of panic.

"Yes you will."

"No I won't, but never mind that now. What's important is that I'm trusting you to look after it. Your father certainly has no interest."

Tears welled in her eyes as she placed the box in Ross's arms. The car horn sounded again.

"Promise me you'll take care of these things. They really are beyond value."

Ross nodded, though he wasn't exactly sure what she meant by that. Pat opened the door for him.

"So will I see you next Saturday?"

"Same as always," he replied.

Out in the car his mother had the radio on loud. Ross climbed in the back seat next to his little sister Rachel, who was still in her leotard from dance class.

"What's in the box?" she asked.

"Just some stuff from Gran's attic – old football kit."

"Sounds smelly," said his mother.

Rachel laughed and stuck her tongue out at Ross. He resisted the temptation to smack her and instead stared out at the passing houses. To think that his great-grandfather had played at Tynecastle all those years ago.

Ross had been to about a dozen Hearts home matches. A friend of his mother from work – Simon – had two season tickets and sometimes invited Ross along. Otherwise he might never have been to a match. Certainly his father wouldn't take him.

Frank Anderson thought football an absurd pursuit. It was one of his favourite dinnertime rants. "Grown men paid millions of pounds for kicking a ball about," he'd huff. "It's just a game. There are countries in Africa worth less than Ronaldo."

Pat said that even as a boy Frank disliked team sports, not being much of an athlete. Ross couldn't recall ever seeing his father break a sweat much less run and kick a ball, but he had no objection to his son playing football. "It's your free time to waste," he'd say. "Just don't expect me to waste mine watching."

On Hearts match days Simon would turn up at the house early for a bacon roll and a cup of tea. He was a big man and completely bald, which made him look a bit like a nightclub bouncer, though he was nothing of the sort. Few people could be more easygoing and friendly than Simon.

After lunch they would set off from the house and down Polwarth Terrace. Here they'd meet the first trickle of other fans bound for the match. By Harrison Road the trickle grew to a throng with people emerging from every side street. Reaching Gorgie the throng swelled into a crowd that choked the pavements as supporters poured from the pubs, having eaten their pies and downed their pints. Ahead, Tynecastle stadium loomed over the tenements like a citadel. On to the turnstiles they'd be swept in a tide of maroon hats and scarves.

But the moment Ross loved most was when he emerged from the dim tunnel through the stand into the bright open arena. Players warming up on the pitch below, music blaring, 18,000 fans in a roar of conversation, the air of hope, expectation – it took his breath away every time. It was like the feeling you get on suddenly coming to the top of a high hill, or the moment on holiday you first reach the beach and find a vast blue ocean spread out at your feet.

3. THE DREAM

Ross stowed the box under his bed as soon as he got home. He didn't want any more awkward questions. But no one mentioned it again, at least not until dinnertime. Saturday was hamburger night and Janet Anderson insisted her family eat together at the dining table. It was Ross's favourite meal and he was starving. He'd wolfed down his own cheeseburger and then began to eye up his little sister's.

"Are you going to finish that?" he asked.

"Maybe," said Rachel.

She slid her plate slowly towards him. "What's it worth to you?"

"Watch out in case he takes your hand with it," said his older sister Kath.

Her plate was empty apart from a thin meat patty and a couple of lettuce leaves. Kath was always on a diet.

"Stop teasing your brother," said Janet.

She reached over with her knife and cut off the nibbled bits from Rachel's burger and put the rest on Ross's plate. Rachel frowned but after a moment or so her eyes grew bright and she glanced slyly up at her brother.

"So what other junk did you and Granny find today?"

Ross kicked her hard under the table. But it was too late; his father had heard.

"Find? Where?"

"Up in the attic," she sang.

Frank lowered his fork.

"You were up in the attic with your grandmother?"

Ross stared down at his plate. Now he'd done it; poor Pat. Might as well take an ad out in *The Scotsman* as tell Rachel anything.

"Answer me!"

"Yes," Ross replied.

"How did you get up there?"

"A ladder."

"Don't be smart. What ladder?"

"One from the shed."

Kath moaned in annoyance.

"Big deal – so they went up to the attic."

Frank stared back at her, incredulous.

"The ceilings in that house must be fourteen feet high and your grandmother is a 78-year-old woman," he said.

Kath flared.

"What's being a woman have to do with it?"

Frank's face grew bright red but he said nothing more.

Later that evening Ross heard him on the phone to Pat.

"Just what were you thinking? Both of you could have broken your necks."

Ross retreated to the sitting room and watched TV for a while but grew so tired he could barely keep his eyes open. So he said goodnight and went upstairs.

Once inside his room he shut the door and reached under his bed for the box. Opening the lid he found the football boots again, buried in among the crumpled newspaper just as before. He took out one of the sheets and smoothed it flat. The banner headline read: "KHRUSHCHEV DEMANDS U.S. APOLOGY" with the date 16 May 1960.

Ross lifted out one of the boots and turned it in his hand. Even he could see the quality – hand-stitched brown leather, tough pliant sole, hammered metal studs. The boot was well scuffed from use but had been carefully cleaned and polished before being packed away.

On a whim he kicked off his slippers and pulled on both boots and tied the waxed cord laces. He stood up and jogged a few steps on the spot. They were stiff and heavy like dress shoes.

He took the rest of the contents from the box and laid them out on his desk. Inside the brown envelope he found the photograph of young Jack Jordan and stuck it up on the wall beside his Hearts calendar. He then pulled on the shorts and the heavy cotton jersey. It hung down to his knees. He looked again at the photograph above his desk. Jack Jordan seemed to grin back at him.

Ross sat down at his desk but felt suddenly exhausted. It was too early to go to bed but he figured a short nap wouldn't hurt. So he kicked off the boots and lay down on his bed. Seconds later it seemed he was fast asleep and dreaming...

He and Jack Jordan were playing football for Hearts at Tynecastle stadium before a large crowd. The men on the terraces wore old style clothes and flat caps. Everything moved in jerky fast motion as if in a silent film reel. Only Jack Jordan sprinted and kicked the ball with fluid grace.

Down the pitch their opponents were in green – Celtic or Hibs – and Ross felt frightened to be playing against grown-up professionals. But Jack smiled with assurance and dribbled the ball across centre midfield. He motioned Ross down the left wing and launched the ball slanting towards the line.

The pass was perfectly paced. Ross caught it on his left foot and drove it down the pitch. He seemed almost to fly rather than run. One of the green defenders rushed in for a tackle but Ross dodged right with a little shuffle and bumped the ball off his heel towards open ground at the centre. Here he took the shot. The ball soared off his boot and curled high over the goalie, dropping just under the crossbar.

A roar exploded from the crowd. Hats flew into the air in celebration. Ross turned to find Jack Jordan sprinting towards him with his arms raised in salute. He grasped Ross warmly by the shoulder and asked, "What's that you're wearing?"

It seemed an odd question and Ross tried to reply. But the words came out all jumbled and the scene before him began to fade. Someone called his name and Ross opened his eyes to find his mother gently poking his shoulder.

"Ross," she repeated. "What are you wearing?"

He rolled over and groaned.

"Just an old football shirt Pat gave me."

"Well, take it off now and get into bed. It's half past eleven."

Ross removed the kit and put on his pyjamas. Janet folded back his covers and turned off the light before kissing his forehead and saying goodnight. Ross nestled under the sheets in hope that if he fell back asleep quickly enough he might rejoin Jack Jordan in that match at old Tynecastle.

4. THE FRIENDLY

Ross awoke early on Monday morning dreading school. The P7 rout by South Morningside would be the talk of the playground that morning. Eating breakfast he was tempted to plead a sore tummy. But he knew it wouldn't fly.

"Fever, vomiting or death," his mother always said when it came to missing school. "No exceptions."

Besides, Janet had a meeting that morning at work she couldn't miss and Frank had already left for the university. Resigned to his fate, Ross gathered his books and said goodbye.

The previous night he'd slept well but had no more dreams of Jack Jordan. He awoke disappointed. The exhilaration of the goal lingered still; it had seemed so real.

Rachel walked ahead up the pavement having met a couple of her friends. But Ross held back, avoiding the inevitable. Another defeat was bad enough but it didn't help that last year's P7 team had gone the entire season unbeaten and taken the Schools' Cup. To make matters even worse, Barry the coach had arranged a friendly for that coming Saturday against the S1 team from Boroughmuir High School, most of whom were former Bruntsfield players.

"It'll be a good chance for you guys to play above your abilities in a supportive atmosphere," he'd said.

"Are you kidding?" Carl Nelson had moaned. "They'll murder us and love every second."

At lunch that day Ross sat with Calum and Ying on the benches near the front gates of the school. A group of S1 boys came along the pavement on their way back from the chippie on Bruntsfield Place. Ross felt his heart sink. Among them was Craig Muir, one of the defenders on the S1 team. Muir had just turned thirteen and already sported a wispy dark moustache on his upper lip. He weighed at least ten stone and though not the quickest on his feet, any lack of speed he made up for in agility and sheer scariness.

"Hey, Anderson. Heard about your stellar performance on Saturday," said Muir.

"Yeah, well, we try to impress," replied Ross.

Muir leaned against the fence.

"So are you looking forward to our friendly?"

"Like the plague," said Ross.

"Hilarious – bet you won't be laughing when I knock you on your butt."

"I'll enjoy the rest."

Ying giggled. Muir glared at him.

"Find that funny, Ying Yang? Heard you've scored more goals this season than Anderson. Too bad they were all for the opposition."

One of the pupil monitors wandered over.

"What's going on guys?"

Muir sneered. "None of your business – grass."

But he did look up to see if a teacher might be watching.

One of his friends moaned, "Come on, Craig. Bell's about to ring."

Muir flicked a chip at Ross.

"See you on the pitch, Anderson."

And they headed down the pavement towards the high school. Ying shook his head.

"We are so stuffed."

"Without question," added Calum.

Ross put his arms around both their shoulders.

"Yeah – but at least it'll be in a 'supportive atmosphere'."

Ross tried his best not to think about the match on Saturday. Besides, he had other things on his mind. He was determined to find out more about Jack Jordan: what position he played, whether he'd scored any goals, how many seasons he was with Hearts.

That night he went up to his room after dinner and switched on his desk lamp. He reached under the bed for Jack's box and pulled out the old brown envelope. Among the contents he found dozens of yellowed newspaper clippings – mainly from *The Scotsman*, some dating back to 1912 but none after 1915. Mostly they were just the week's results and league tables along with short reports of the main First Division matches. He scanned a few but found no mention of Jack.

Scattered among the clippings were some old football programmes. He opened one from a match with Hibernian on 5 December 1914. Across the middle-page spread was a photograph of the squad – three rows of men, kneeling, sitting, standing, with a bowler-hatted manager to one side. He scanned the players' names: Willie Wilson, Alfred Briggs, Duncan Currie, Harry Wattie, Bob Preston, Tom Gracie – but no Jack.

Just as he was about to give up, Ross came upon a page torn from a newspaper called *The Scottish Football Gazette*. A paragraph was circled near the bottom with a second team result and short summary:

HEART OF MIDLOTHIAN "A", 3; DUNDEE "A", 1. Brisk, wet afternoon; young Jack Jordan continues to show promise for Hearts reserves, scoring two – one off a wayward pass from Wilson...

And on another clipping:

HEART OF MIDLOTHIAN "A", 5; DUNDEE "A", 0.
Jordan dominates Hearts side with three goals; two in the first half...

Ross found a dozen more such results, each mentioning Jack Jordan by name and always as top scorer. Reading the long forgotten pages he felt an odd flush of pride. His great-grandfather had been a star striker, even if not for the first team.

Sorting through the rest of the newspaper clippings he found another, but this one wasn't from the sports pages. It was a group photograph of young men in street clothes under the headline: "HEARTS ENLIST". Ross studied the faces and there on the second row, third from the left, stood Jack Jordan.

That night Ross had another dream of being at Tynecastle stadium, but this time he was watching a regular league match in the present day. He sat in one of the season-ticket seats but without Simon. A capacity crowd filled the stadium and down on the pitch the tiger mascots Teenie and Tynie conducted the crowd in "Hearts, Hearts, Glorious Hearts". Over in the far stand a tight square of opposition fans waved green scarves and hats and chanted, although completely drowned out. A man next to Ross cupped his hands to his mouth and shouted, "Dinnae even try!"

Time seemed compressed as it does in dreams, and down at the entrance to the players' tunnel, officials in fluorescent yellow vests began to rush about. An announcer broke in: "We're pleased to welcome some very special guests at today's match. Please give a Tynecastle cheer to some Hearts heroes of old."

Out of the tunnel jogged a squad of footballers dressed in the same old-fashioned kit as in Jack's box.

But unlike the colourful scene around them they were pale and grey like ghosts. Just as before, the players moved with odd jerky motion like in an old silent film. Last to emerge from the tunnel was Jack Jordan.

Ross shouted in excitement to the fans seated around him.

"Hey! That's my great-grandfather down there."

He knew it sounded ridiculous. Not one of the players was over the age of thirty. But nobody around him listened or even seemed to notice. They munched chips or texted on their mobiles.

Ross grabbed the arm of the man next to him.

"Look!"

The guy grinned quizzically and Ross realised then he was still wearing his pyjamas.

Down on the pitch the ghost players formed a circle and began to perform an odd, regimented passing drill – weaving quickly among themselves with a dozen brown leather balls in constant motion. It looked like slapstick comedy. People began to laugh and cheer. The fans around Ross looked up.

"Who are those guys?" someone asked.

But just then a huge roar arose from the crowd. Down at the mouth of the players' tunnel the real

Hearts squad had appeared, dressed in white jerseys and bright maroon shorts. Everyone jumped to their feet and the announcer cried, "Come on you Jambos! Let's make some noise!"

The Hearts players thundered out of the tunnel across the pitch. In that instant Jack Jordan and the rest of the ghost squad vanished as though already forgotten.

On Saturday morning Ross shovelled down his porridge as Ying waited to chum him down to Harrison Park for a 9.30 kick-off. Finishing his breakfast, he found his kit bag at the front door as usual but no football boots.

"Anyone seen my boots?" he hollered.

"Ask me another," his mother replied.

And then Ross remembered. It had been so muddy last Saturday, Pat had given him a plastic bag for his boots. He must have left the bag in her porch. He'd never get there and back to the training ground in time for kick-off. Just then another thought occurred to him.

Ross dashed upstairs and down the hall to his room. He reached under his bed for the old leather boots and then descended the steps two at a time, stuffing them into his kit bag. He and Ying sprinted down Polwarth Terrace towards the park.

Ross had never been superstitious. Notions of good or bad fortune didn't figure much in his thinking. But it had been an odd week and hurrying then to the match he began to wonder if wearing the boots that morning might just bring him luck.

Only a few spectators had turned up to watch the match. Ross felt a little ridiculous when he sat on the sidelines to lace up the boots. Barry at least was impressed.

"Those certainly look vintage," he said, having himself opted that morning for a dark wool pinstripe suit, which made him look like a Chicago gangster.

Craig Muir and the other S1s were less admiring.

"Hey, Anderson, get your boots from Oxfam?" Muir called.

Everyone on the pitch laughed but the grass was wet and Ross figured the boots would at least be better than trainers.

The opening whistle blew and the P7s took first possession. But within a few seconds the S1s had the ball and their centre forward broke free of the defence and made a neat side step around Ying to score the first goal. Things didn't get any better after that.

Kicking off again after a second S1 goal – scored from a corner – Calum passed the ball to Owen at centre midfield, who eluded a couple of players before booting it hard down the left wing towards Ross.

It was an excellent pass, perfectly timed. Ross sprinted down the line to run on to the ball. The boots felt stiff and ungainly. But he managed to check the pass off his inside foot and drive it forward. Looking up he glimpsed Muir hurtling towards him.

Scary as this was Ross saw an opportunity; the big defender's momentum would make it hard to change direction. So Ross dodged left and cut back inside. Muir brushed past his shoulder with a curse.

A cheer rose from the parents on the sidelines. Nothing stood now between Ross and the goalie but open ground. He drove the ball towards the centre, looking for position. The goalie came forward with a frantic wave of his arms.

"Have a dig. Shoot!" Bob Nelson hollered.

Ross turned on the ball. It was an easy chip. He'd

made countless similar shots in practice. He planted his right foot, but as he followed through, the toe of his left boot scuffed over the pitch, and he stumbled and fell forward into the grass. The ball trickled to the edge of the box.

"Smooth," said the goalie and punted the ball back to Muir.

Ross picked himself slowly off the ground. The rest of the match passed in a blur. He hardly touched the ball again. Over and over the moment replayed in his head like some sick video loop. The final whistle blew and Ross walked off the far end of the pitch.

"Come shake hands," he heard Barry call, but Ross kept on walking. It wasn't "sporting", he knew, but he simply couldn't bear facing Muir. He found a bench alongside the canal and changed out of the muddy boots.

"Some luck," he muttered.

Crossing the bridge, he felt tempted to toss his kit bag over the side and forget football altogether.

At Pat's he called glumly at the open front door, "It's me."

"You're early," she replied from the kitchen and came out into the hallway.

"Is everything okay?"

But before he could answer she spotted the muddy football boots hanging by their knotted laces over the top of his kit bag.

"What are those?" she asked.

Ross turned away. Pat reached out and yanked the kit bag from his shoulder. Her eyes flared in anger.

"Have you been playing football in these?"

"So what if I have?" Ross snapped back. "It's just some old boots."

She stared at him for a moment in disbelief.

"Maybe I was wrong to have trusted you," she said, and then turned and walked back into the kitchen.

Ross stood a moment alone in the hallway deep in regret. He then sighed and followed her. Pat stood at the sink with the boots on the draining board.

"I'm sorry," he muttered.

"Put the gas on under that pot of milk," she replied and began to fill the sink.

Ross sat at the table and watched in silence as she used a wet cloth to carefully daub the mud and grass from the boots. Afterwards she stuffed the insides with crumpled newspaper and left them to dry by the radiator. By then the milk had boiled. She whisked two tall mugs of hot chocolate and sat down at the table opposite Ross.

"Let me tell you something about those boots," she said. "And your great-grandfather."

5. THE PERFECT FIT

A good pair of football boots did not come cheap in 1914 – especially not for a brewery worker with a family of four. Tom Jordan brought home less than two guineas a week from his job at Fountain Brewery. The few coins left over after expenses – rent, groceries, coal – went into a tea tin kept on a high shelf above the range. Here the family banked their savings for summer holidays by the sea at Dunbar.

That first Saturday morning after Jack got his letter from Tynecastle, Tom retrieved the tin, but instead of depositing money he poured the contents out onto the kitchen table and counted out 25 shillings. Jack tried to protest; his old boots had at least another season's wear. But Tom would not be persuaded.

"I won't have my son taking the pitch at Tynecastle in some ratty hand-me-downs."

"Jack Jordan Esq" – the letter had been addressed. It offered a six-month contract and had been signed by the manager himself, John McCartney. He had approached Jack after a match in which he'd scored three goals against Dalry Primrose.

A gruff man in a bowler hat and three-piece suit, he handed Jack a card and said, "Come down to Gorgie Road for a chat."

Jack had been so dumbstruck that his father had to answer for him.

"Certainly. Delighted, Mr McCartney."

To play for Hearts had been Jack's one ambition since the age of seven when his father took him to his first match. Now at seventeen he was being offered a trial with the second team at centre forward. It seemed unreal, like a dream from which he'd soon wake up.

Certainly no one would have predicted that Jack would one day play professional football. He had been a frail child, asthmatic and prone to chest infections. Many a night he spent tented under a blanket with a steaming kettle to ease his breathing.

The doctor had told his mother, "He'll never make a runner; hasn't the lungs for it."

But despite such predictions and his parents' worries, Jack did little but run. Among a gang of children he played tig and street football on the cobbled lanes and drying greens shadowed by the tall tenement buildings of Fountainbridge. Often he'd collapse gasping for breath and a child would run for his mother or his older sister Mary to carry him home.

"I'm okay," he'd say. "Just a wee bit winded."

Over the years the asthma eased in severity and his father allowed Jack to play for Shandon Boys. Here he demonstrated both speed and agility on the pitch – first at midfield and then as a striker. The manager at Shandon told Tom that Jack had an instinctive feel for the game, something that couldn't be taught.

To Jack being in motion with a ball just seemed natural – legs, lungs, head all came together. He could no more account for it than explain the beating of his own heart.

That Saturday morning in late June, Jack and his father took the number 23 tram down to an athletics outfitter on Thistle Street. Here Tom asked to see the best football boots in the shop. The sales clerk looked doubtful but brought out a pair from the back.

"You won't get better than these," he said, laying the boots on the counter. "Top quality stitching, fine English leather."

"How much?" Tom asked.

"Twenty-two shillings," replied the clerk.

Jack whispered at his father's back, "We can't afford that."

"Fit him a pair," Tom replied without hesitation.

Jack protested again but sat on the bench and let the clerk measure his feet. The new boots were stiff and springy but the perfect fit. Jack stood up and took a few steps and then a hop. It was as though he had a whole new pair of feet.

Later to celebrate the purchase they went for lunch at Mathers. Workers had just come off a shift at one of the mills and the pub was loud and smoky. They found two stools and Jack felt he'd never seen his father look happier sitting at the bar beside him eating his steak pie and chips.

"Thanks again for the boots," Jack said.

Tom raised his pint and shouted to be heard over the noise of the pub, "I may have bought them, but it's you that has to fill them."

Jack turned up for his first training session that next Monday along with two other new players. Drew Hendry had been recruited from a local club at Mossend – a tall, lanky goalkeeper. The other man came all the way from Newcastle. A scout acting for McCartney spotted Hugh Wilson playing winger for an amateur side in Jarrow. He'd been working as a miner before giving up his job to come north to Edinburgh.

Trainer Jimmy Duckworth met them at the gate for a quick tour of the grounds before assigning each a locker. Jack had played against Mossend before so he and Hendry chatted while changing into their kit. Wilson spoke not a word, a grim, unsmiling boy with badly pockmarked cheeks.

All three jogged across the training pitch to join the other second team players warming up. The squad spent an hour at drills and then the assistant trainer Alex Lyon split them up for a match.

Jack played at centre forward but struggled to find the measure of the game. The defenders were far more confident and aggressive than he was used to – not surprisingly. It was a whole different level of football. Try as he might he could not force an opening near the box.

Word had already spread among the squad that McCartney had recruited yet another Englishman. Some players resented this and one in particular – a defender named Bryson – seemed to take an instant hatred to Hugh Wilson.

All through the first half the older player bumped and jostled the Englishman, keeping him off balance. Each time Wilson got near the ball Bryson was there for the tackle, but always with an added shoulder or elbow. Lyon warned him half a dozen times but it made no difference.

Wilson took the abuse without comment and about ten minutes into the second half the ball came to him again. Bryson charged in, but this time Wilson made a neat side step and turned on the ball, leaving the defender nothing but thin air. He dribbled down towards the corner in position for a cross. Bryson was so enraged by this he charged in from behind with a brutal blind tackle that swept Wilson off his feet. He landed hard on his shoulder.

Bryson walked off the pitch without waiting to be

told. McCartney later suspended him for a week. Wilson rose slowly and Jack jogged over to help him up.

"That was dirty," he said.

But Wilson ignored the outstretched hand and spat.

"Had worse done to me."

"Fair enough," Jack replied and turned away thinking, *Misery guts.*

Wilson missed the free kick but soon took possession again for an attack up the right wing. Jack scrambled for position at the centre and spotted an opening. He shouted though hardly expected to get the pass. In that instant Wilson cut across from the line and lofted the ball just ahead of Jack a few yards outside the box. Jack struck as it landed and the shot rocketed off his boot past the keeper and into the net.

A hearty cheer rose from the players and Jack turned to find Wilson approaching with a grin.

"Nice shot," said the English player.

"Nicely delivered," Jack replied.

And with that very first goal the two footballers formed an effective duo. In the opening match of the season against Raith Rovers reserve team, Jack would score two goals both off the boot of Hugh

Wilson. In the next dozen matches it would be much the same.

Off the pitch Jack soon realised that what he'd first taken for arrogance in the English player was mostly shyness. Hugh had stepped off the train from Newcastle without knowing a single person in Edinburgh. McCartney helped him find a job in the brewery washing floors. On the little wages he earned Hugh rented a room in a damp basement flat off Dalry Road. Here he subsisted mainly on cold tinned beans and bread.

Jack's mother was horrified when he told her this one morning over breakfast.

"You get that boy around here for a solid meal," she demanded.

The next evening Hugh came home with Jack after training and Mrs Jordan made a steaming fish pie with cabbage and tatties. Hugh had three helpings and then steamed pudding and custard.

"Sorry," he said between mouthfuls. "It's just so good."

But Mrs Jordan was delighted.

"So is all your family in Newcastle?" she asked.

Hugh put down his fork.

"Well, it's just me and Dad back home now. My

little sister lives in Durham with my Aunt Bell. Mum died two years ago."

"How sad for you," said Jack's sister Mary.

"Yeah, considering that Dad must be the worst cook on Tyneside."

"I imagine he misses you," she added.

"It'll be a quiet house now – that's for sure. But he wanted me to come. Dad used to play football for Jarrow but had to give it up at fifteen to dig coal. He told me to take my chance while I could – not as though the pit'll be going anywhere."

From that night on Hugh Wilson took most of his evening meals with the Jordans. He tried to offer money for his share of the food but Tom refused. Some nights when Mary's fiancé George joined the family, there were six around the small kitchen table. On Saturdays Hugh and Jack would go out after tea either to a theatre if they had a spare shilling or to the Palace Dancehall. Here they'd eye up girls across the wide polished floor but rarely pluck up the courage to ask for a waltz or a polka.

Had either of them picked up a newspaper on 29 June 1914, it's doubtful they would have given much thought to the headlines announcing that Archduke Franz Ferdinand had been felled by an assassin's bullet in Sarajevo. Too much else was happening in their busy lives. Nor could they have predicted the sequence of events over the coming weeks and months – the tangle of alliances that later in August would lead Britain to war.

6. THE GREATER GAME

Hearts first team opened the 1914 season on 15 August with a match against the defending champions Celtic. A crowd of 18,000 spectators packed the stadium at Tynecastle. Jack had managed to get a free ticket for his father and together with Hugh they sat in the centre of the main stand.

The crowd buzzed with excitement. Hopes were high that season for winning the league. McCartney had fielded the strongest squad in years – evident from the first whistle. In minutes, forward Tom Gracie just missed going one up on a superb cross from winger Harry Wattie. Jack watched in wonder, trying to imagine how he could ever hope to play football in such company.

Hugh shook his head in dismay as if reading Jack's mind.

Tom Jordan laughed.

"Come on boys. Have some confidence."

Just before half-time Wattie drove in the first goal. The crowd jumped to its feet with a roar. A minute later the whistle blew and Jack went in search of three hot pies.

Below the stand he passed a table of women taking a collection for soldiers in Europe. Eleven days before, the German army had invaded Belgium, and Britain had declared war. Jack found a kiosk and queued for the pies. Returning to his seat he lingered a moment passing the table in order to read the poster: "Duty Calls! Give to the Prince of Wales Relief Fund".

One of the women called out, "Young man! What are you doing here?"

Jack turned to see if she was addressing someone else – a plump elderly lady in a starched white blouse, her white hair pulled back in a tight bun.

"No. I mean you with the pies. Why are you here today?"

Jack shrugged.

"To watch football."

"Yes. I can see that," she replied. "And do you think this a worthwhile thing to do?"

A few of the ladies at the table looked away in mirth but the old woman was stern and unsmiling. Others in the passing crowd paused to listen. Jack was unsure how to reply.

"I don't..." But she cut him off.

"Do you know there may be British soldiers dying as we speak? You should be occupying yourself with more serious matters than watching football. There is a greater game and it can be found on the fields of Belgium and France."

Jack turned and hurried away.

"Wait," she called. "I'm not finished..."

Tom sensed Jack's agitation when he returned with the pies.

"Something wrong?" he asked.

"No," Jack replied.

But he had been shaken by the old woman's words. Similar statements had been published in the newspapers – even calls to postpone the football season. The Scottish Football Association had resisted. A swift end to the war was expected and the SFA felt such a move would only add to public panic. Jack had not thought of this as being his war. After all, he was only just out of school.

Later that afternoon the trio shoved their way into Diggers along with over a hundred other fans crowding the pub in celebration of Hearts two-nil victory over Celtic. Gracie had scored the second goal from a long drive from outside the box. Beer sloshed from their pint glasses into the damp sawdust with barely elbowroom to take a sip. The air was hot and fumed with sweat.

Tom Jordan shouted over the noise, "Looks like this could be Hearts' year – barring any disaster."

But Jack was distracted. He could still hear the woman's voice in his head – more serious matters, soldiers dying as we speak.

"What about the war?" he asked.

"War?" said Tom. "No need to worry about that now that Britain's shown the Kaiser we won't be pushed around. The politicians'll sort it out."

"Newspapers are already talking about conscription," said Hugh.

Tom shook his head. "It'll never happen. I wager our troops will be back home well before Christmas."

But Jack wasn't convinced.

Over the next weeks Jack carried on with his busy life – working days as a trainee clerk at the North British Rubber Company and then rushing off in the evenings for training at Gorgie Road. But almost everywhere he went a whiskered Lord Kitchener pointed out at him from leaflets and posters declaring:

BRITONS

YOUR COUNTRY NEEDS

YOU

Newspapers with bold headlines told of British and French troops in heroic battles at Marne and Ypres to prevent the German army reaching the French channel ports. But in many ways life went on as usual – including football. On 31 October a crowd of over 10,000 fans turned out to watch Hearts defeat Ayr United, while in Glasgow over 40,000 watched Celtic defeat Rangers in the first Old Firm match of the season.

Many people considered it an outrage to carry on playing and watching games while men fought and died. Letters published in newspapers condemned clubs and players alike. To Jack it just seemed unfair. Having worked all his life to achieve this one ambition, all he felt now was shame – as did most of the Hearts players. He had heard that a group of women in town had formed a "League of the White Feather". In their handbags they carried an envelope containing goose feathers collected from butcher shops and old down pillows. Any man met on the street who was of fighting age and out of uniform would be presented with a feather as a mark of his cowardice and lack of patriotism.

Manager McCartney also took the criticisms to heart. One afternoon a notice appeared in the changing rooms to announce mandatory drill sessions for all playing staff to prepare for possible military service. Jack and Hugh turned up for the first session at Grindlay Street Hall. A reserve back named Annan Ness was put in charge, being the only player on the team with any experience at soldiering.

That first night they drilled with field hockey sticks in place of rifles, and Ness had trouble convincing the other players that the exercise was anything more than a lark. They took to calling him the "Sergeant Major" but paid little attention when he gave instructions, much less orders. Worst among them was Pat Crossan, another defender on the first team.

Crossan was one of the most popular players on the squad, a superb all-round athlete, said by sports writers to be the fastest man in Scotland over one hundred yards. Hearts female supporters swooned over his tall good looks, to the annoyance of the other players who dubbed him "the handsomest man in the world".

Crossan treated the drill sessions as a joke. Should Ness order, "To the left face!" he would turn right and stand nose-to-nose with the man next to him. And when Ness called, "About face!" he'd take one step forward and stand stiff at attention nearly kissing the man in front.

Ness would plead, "Come on, Pat. This isn't exactly my idea of fun either."

Crossan would then look contrite. "Sorry, Annan. I'll get the hang of it soon. Promise!"

To further support the war effort, the club also allowed recruiting officers to set up tables at Tynecastle on match days to enlist volunteers. Only a trickle of men signed up and among them was a reserve centre forward for Hearts called Jimmy Speedie – an insurance clerk who Jack knew as an older boy at Boroughmuir High School.

But such measures were not enough to satisfy the club's critics. One day a letter appeared in the Edinburgh Evening News signed "Soldier's Daughter" which read, "While Hearts continue to play football, enabled to pursue their peaceful play by the sacrifice of thousands of their countrymen, they might adopt, temporarily, a nom de plume, say 'The White Feathers of Midlothian'."

Jack felt he could no longer bear the indignity and resolved to enlist at the Royal Scots recruiting office on Castle Street. He told Hugh of his plans one evening on the way home from training.

"We could join up together."

Hugh said nothing for a few moments. It was a cold night in November. A fine but steady drizzle soaked their clothes.

"I'm not sure I want to join," Hugh finally replied. "Or at least not as a volunteer. Seems to me from reading newspapers it's mainly politicians and rich men behind this war. Lord This and Sir That with their pits and their mills and their factories. But when it comes to the fighting and dying it's not them going to France."

"But how can you stand being called a coward?" said Jack.

"Maybe it's more cowardly to join up just because someone tells you to," he replied.

So Jack remained torn. But soon another opportunity arose – one that would silence all the cranks and critics.

7. A HEARTS BATTALION

The first Jack heard of it was one evening after training at Gorgie Road. McCartney called all the players together into the dressing room. He stood up on a bench and removed his hat.

"There's no need for me to remind you all of what the newspapers are publishing these days about the professional game," he said. "Rot – pure and simple. I don't like it and neither does the Board."

A roar of agreement filled the room. McCartney raised his hand for silence.

"Well, in the past few days an opportunity has arisen to do something about it. Edinburgh already has one battalion preparing to join the British Expeditionary

Force in France. Now a second city battalion is being raised by a long-time Hearts supporter, Sir George McCrae. He needs to enlist over a thousand men and has approached the directors with the idea of appealing for volunteers under the banner of Heart of Midlothian – a battalion of Tynecastle supporters to train and fight together."

The men cheered and McCartney waited again for quiet.

"But to make the plan work," he continued, "Sir George needs players to rally support. So the Board has agreed to keep paying full wages to anyone who enlists, as long as he's able to play football in the regular season, and half wages when unable due to military service. This comes with an agreement to re-engage any player on original terms if fit and well upon return from the conflict. So I'm here to ask: will you join and serve king and country?"

Jack rose to his feet without hesitation, along with most of the other players. Hugh had been sitting next to him on the bench and looked up white-faced.

"Come on – a Hearts battalion!" urged Jack.

Slowly Hugh stood up as well.

That night over supper Jack said nothing to his parents. He knew how his mother would react – anger then tears, a dozen reasons for not going. He saw no point in arguing about it now.

Next day at training Sir George sent along a physician to check that all the volunteers were fit for service. Jack waited his turn in the line but decided not to mention his childhood asthma as the doctor listened to his heart and chest. Certainly if he could play football he was fit enough to be a soldier.

An appeal was published that week in all the local newspapers along with the announcement of a grand rally to be held on Friday night at the Usher Hall.

TO THE YOUNG MEN OF EDINBURGH
The present crisis is one of extreme gravity. World-wide issues are trembling in the balance. I appeal with confidence to the patriotism and generous enthusiasm of my fellow citizens... All cannot go, but if your home ties permit, and you shirk your obvious duty, you may escape a hero's death, but you will go through your life feeling mean. In the presence of the God of Battles, ask of your conscience this question: DARE I STAND ASIDE?

Jack read that morning's *The Scotsman* sitting out by the canal eating the sandwich his mother had packed. A hero's death, he thought to himself. It sounded like something out of Greek legend – the Spartan borne from battle upon his own shield. Except there were no shields now, only a telegram from the War Office notifying the family that a son or father had been killed or was missing in action. A few families in Fountainbridge had already received such telegrams.

Yet the newspapers still spoke of a quick end to the war. Jack figured chances were he wouldn't even see action – though he hoped not. Otherwise what was the point of being a soldier?

Staring into the murky water of the canal he tried to imagine his mother receiving such a telegram. Sitting with her cup of tea at the kitchen table, the knock at the door, her opening it to the uniformed boy, envelope in his hand... but here he pushed the image from his mind. Lunchtime was over and the chief clerk would already be looking for him to distribute the afternoon post.

Jack had never been inside the Usher Hall before – the massive ornate concert venue in the shadow of Edinburgh Castle. That Friday night it was filled to capacity with a crowd of over 4,000. Young men upon entering the doors were presented with an enlistment form and a copy of the appeal. Jack sat up on the stage with the rest of the Hearts players and a host of Edinburgh dignitaries, listening to speaker after speaker. Lords, MPs, professors – all of them urging the young, strong and fit "not to stand back from the fray".

A mighty cheer arose for the last speaker to approach the lectern – Lieutenant Colonel Sir George McCrae. He was in his fifties then, a distinguished looking man with greying hair and a thick moustache. Sir George had been born in poverty to a housemaid but had earned his fortune in Edinburgh as a "hatter and hosier" before being elected an MP to Westminster. He had also been a soldier with the Royal Scots.

As the Colonel reached into his jacket for the sheet bearing his speech, someone in the audience shouted, "Well done, Sir George."

But he didn't smile, just stared out over the

audience and said, "This is not a night for titles. I stand before you humbly as a fellow Scot. Nothing more and nothing less. You know I don't speak easily of crisis, but this is what confronts us..."

He then set out in simple terms his commission from Lord Kitchener to raise the battalion and his pledge to lead it in the field.

"I would not – I could not – ask you to serve unless I share the danger at your side," he said. "In a moment I will walk down to Castle Street and set my name to the list of volunteers. Who will join me?"

And with that Sir George left the stage and walked up the aisle and out the door, bound for the battalion recruitment office at the Palace Hotel. By midnight over 300 men had been added to the ranks.

Jack made his way home after the Usher Hall emptied and when he entered the flat he saw a light still burning in the kitchen. Both his parents sat grim faced – a copy of the *Evening News* open on the table. Above a large group photograph read the headline:

HEARTS ENLIST

His mother's eyes were red and bloodshot. Tom Jordan just looked dead tired, almost defeated.

"I suppose you meant to tell us sometime," he said and rose to put the kettle on the range.

8. THE SILVER BADGE

Ross heard the familiar toot of the car horn outside. His mother would be waiting at the front gate to collect him.

"So what happened next?" he asked. "Did Jack go to war?"

"Sorry," said Pat. "I'll finish the story another time."

Ross groaned and made her promise to tell him more next Saturday. Saying goodbye at the front door Pat handed him back the clean leather football boots without comment.

Sunday evening after dinner Ross lay on the floor of the sitting room watching TV with his sisters. During the adverts he turned to his father who sat in a chair reading *The Times*.

"Can you remember your grandfather?" Ross asked.

"Which one?" Frank Anderson replied without looking up from the newspaper.

"Pat's dad – Jack."

"No. He died the same year I was born."

"And that was 1960?"

"Yes."

"Did you know he enlisted in the army during World War I?"

Frank sighed and lowered his newspaper. "Most men in his generation did."

He then peered over his reading glasses. "Have you and Granny been making more forays up in that attic?"

"No," said Ross.

"Good. Glad to hear it," he replied and sank back behind his paper.

Ross grew bored and went upstairs to his room. He sat down at his desk and turned on the lamp. Jack Jordan gazed out as always from his spot on the wall by the Hearts calendar, but there was something different about him. The face in the photograph seemed somehow transformed, brought to life by Pat's words. Behind those grey eyes now lay hopes and fears and ambitions before absent. Ross found it both curious and sad.

That next morning he awoke early with the idea already in his head. He reached under the bed for Jack's chest and found the cardboard jewellery box containing the silver badge. Pulling a jumper over his pyjamas he quietly slipped out his bedroom door.

No one would be awake for another half-hour at least. Ross sneaked down the stairs and into the small room that served as his parents' study. In the dim light he found the switch to the desktop computer. The monitor bathed the walls in a green glow.

Ross laid the box next to the computer and opened the internet browser to Google. In the prompt he typed the inscription from the badge: "For King and Empire – Services Rendered".

The search returned dozens of hits. He clicked one near the top from the National Archives. Here he found both an image and description of the badge. The text said it dated from World War I, 1914–1918, and was called the Silver War Badge. It was given to "all military personnel discharged as a result of sickness or wounds contracted or received during the war".

His great-grandfather had been a soldier in the First World War. And this medal meant he had been injured. Why hadn't Pat mentioned this before?

He heard the bathroom door upstairs creak and the splash of water in the shower. Switching off the computer, he put the badge back into the box and tucked it under his jumper, unsure why he felt the need to hide his discovery. He had so many questions for Pat next Saturday.

Later that morning going to school, Ross again dreaded the grief he'd get over his performance at

Saturday's game, but nobody mentioned it all day. Not, at least, until he and Ying were heading back from the shop after school for badminton practice.

Walking down the broad avenue towards the front of Bruntsfield Primary he spotted Craig Muir and two other boys approaching in the opposite direction. It was too late to cross the road.

"Well, look here. It's our star striker, Anderson," Muir called. "Sorry we didn't get a chance to shake hands after the game on Saturday."

The three older boys blocked the pavement with Muir in the centre.

"So why did you run off so quickly?" he asked.

"I had somewhere to go," Ross replied.

"Home to cry in your pillow?"

The boys laughed. Ross grabbed Ying and tried to push past them.

"Hold on," said Muir, catching his jacket. "I only wanted to congratulate you on that amazing missed goal."

"Much appreciated," Ross replied. "But we're late."

Muir looked down.

"I see you're not still wearing the lace-up granny boots. What was that all about? Are they your lucky boots? Hate to break it to you pal – they don't work."

"Well, at least I managed to get past you," said Ross.

Muir's face darkened.

"I tripped."

"No," said Ross. "I tripped – in front of the goal, having left you behind."

"Are you calling me a liar?" said Muir.

"Not unless you're telling a lie."

Ross never expected the punch – a swift jab to the nose. Pain exploded in a burst of red before his closed eyes. He bent over double and felt he might be sick.

Ying shouted and then there was another voice. A young woman had come out into the front garden of one of the flats.

"Stop that now or I'll call the police."

When Ross looked up again Muir and the other boys were already hurrying off up the pavement. He pulled his hand away from his nose and saw blood. The woman went into her flat and came back out with a wad of paper towels.

"Will you be okay?" she asked. "Can I call your parents?"

"No, thanks," said Ross. "I'm fine."

But he wasn't. When he and Ying got to the school gates Ross decided to skip practice that day.

"Think I'll head home and get cleaned up," he said.

"Can I chum you?" asked Ying.

"No. You go on in."

"What if you meet them again?"

"I'll run."

But Ross managed to avoid Muir and his pals on the walk home. Reaching the front door he pulled out his key. All the windows were dark as both his sisters had after-school clubs and his parents wouldn't be back from work for hours. Ross felt he couldn't bear the silence.

Pat opened her door and peered out first in surprise and then shock.

"What happened to you?"

Blood had crusted around Ross's nose and stained his white school shirt.

"Come in," she said and gently pushed him down the hall into the kitchen.

Here Pat soaked a dishcloth with warm water and wiped the blood from his face. She insisted he remove the shirt for washing and found an old bathrobe for him to wear. Ross then told her what had happened with Muir.

"Will I call the high school?" she asked.

"No. It'll just make things worse," Ross replied.

"Okay. But you'll have to tell your parents about it."

"Why? Dad won't care – at least not about me," said Ross. "He'll just go mental: 'Nobody punches *my* kid!'"

Pat sighed.

"I know it might seem like that sometimes, but he cares more than you imagine. Trust me – I've been putting up with his bluster for the last thirty years. Maybe he could be a little less grumpy some of the time but sadly you can't choose your father – or your son."

And they both laughed.

Pat then placed a saucepan of milk on the gas ring and brought out a dish of digestive biscuits. But Ross wasn't hungry.

"I went onto the computer and found out more about the silver badge in Jack's box. Was he wounded in the war?"

"Yes," Pat replied.

"Was it bad?"

She took a deep breath.

"Not as bad as some."

"Could you maybe tell me more?" asked Ross. "Seeing as I'm here."

Pat turned away to the stove and said, "I can tell you what I know."

9. COME WITH US TO FRANCE

A vast crowd blocked George Street that December morning. Jack stood in one of two long columns of men over 1,200 strong, all in heavy overcoats as it was bitterly cold. He carried with him a holdall with extra shirts and underwear and also a shaving kit he barely had need of. Dozens of police constables made futile attempts to keep the crush of family and well-wishers away from the men. Jack had long lost sight of his father.

Sir George McCrae surveyed the chaos from a tall chestnut horse. He was in full uniform with a holster and pistol at his belt. He kept check of the time with a pocket watch and at the stroke of noon signalled to his sergeant major. Two bands from the Royal Scots struck up *Scotland the Brave* and the battalion set off towards Charlotte Square with the men shuffling to the beat of the drums. As they marched back down the broad thoroughfare of Princes Street, a mob of young boys ran to keep pace with the pipers.

Upon reaching Waverley Market the men fell out and were provided a free lunch. Jack joined a long queue of men before a row of tables where waiters in white aprons served warm steak pies and cups of tea. Reaching the front he met up with Hugh, mouth stuffed with a pie, another in his hand.

"Not bad, this," he said.

"See you saved one for me," replied Jack.

"Don't worry, there's plenty."

Jack had not taken his first bite when the officers began blowing whistles. All the men were reassembled in lines and marched across town to George Heriot's School. Here temporary battalion headquarters had been set up in the grounds, with the examination hall and art classrooms fitted out as barracks along with four floors of an abandoned brewery building adjacent to the school playground.

Chaos again ensued as the men crowded before a large bulletin board with lists detailing where they had been assigned. The battalion was organised into four "companies" with men serving alongside pals and workmates – distillery and brewery men, bankers and civil servants, students and teachers, printers and typesetters. Jack and Hugh were assigned to "C company" along with other sportsmen, including Hearts players and professional and junior footballers from Hibernian, Raith Rovers, Falkirk, Mossend and numerous local clubs. All were to share a billet on the third floor of the brewery building, which had been furnished with trestle beds along with communal sinks and flushing latrines.

Tea was a noisy affair in the large exam hall. Jack sat with Hugh and Crossan and a few other players on a bench eating large plates of salty Irish stew.

"Looks like they at least intend feeding us," grumbled Crossan.

"Cheer up, Pat," said Annan Ness. "Just think how irresistible you'll look in uniform."

"Well, there is that," he replied. "Maybe a smart red tunic."

Harry Wattie shook his head.

"Good thing you can pass a ball, Crossan, because you couldn't pass a mirror if you tried."

It was an old joke but everyone laughed.

Later that night Jack had trouble sleeping on the lumpy straw mattress. The air was stale and someone in one of the adjacent beds snored loudly. He had only ever spent a few nights away from home – a week with the Scouts in Pitlochry, a choral festival in Glasgow. This time he didn't know when he might sleep in his own bed again.

At 6.00 am they were roused by a bugle call and a bawling sergeant: "Come on – show a leg." A few jokers obliged by sticking a foot out from under their blankets and had to be turfed out of bed.

A quick wash at the sinks and breakfast was followed by assembly on the Heriot's playground. Here the men were instructed in the basics of drill. Jack and the footballers had an advantage from the evening sessions at Grindlay Street. But the rest of the men formed at best a disordered rabble, despite much shouting and abuse from the drill sergeants.

After lunch the entire battalion set out on a route march through Swanston Village into the Pentland Hills. Again the footballers performed well, being in top fitness, but other men struggled.

Climbing a steep section of path, Jack and Hugh passed a boy throwing up in a clump of gorse. Jack recognised him – a fellow named Albert Ripley who was also in the sportsmen company, though he looked a most unlikely athlete: short and slight with thinning straw hair and thick round glasses.

"You okay?" Jack asked.

Ripley gasped for breath. "Must have been something I ate."

"Obviously," said Hugh, trying not to laugh.

They helped him up and waited as he caught his breath.

"Better get a move on," said Jack. "That sergeant will roast us otherwise."

Soon the three reached a high ridge overlooking Edinburgh below. Jack had never seen the city laid out like this at his feet: Castle Hill and the jumble of churches and stone tenements stretching down the Royal Mile to Holyrood Palace and the grassy slopes of Arthur's seat and Salisbury Crags; beyond that the blue sea of the Forth.

"Not a shabby view," said Hugh, catching his breath.

"Not at all," replied Jack.

Ripley could only manage a wheeze. But on the way back down the hill he felt much better and kept up a steady chatter. He told Jack and Hugh about his schooling at George Watson's College and how he'd been training to be a lawyer before the war broke out. He didn't play football but was Hearts daft and claimed to have never missed a match in the last seven years. Ripley could quote almost any Hearts statistics in any season you could name – ranking, win-loss-draw, even who scored what against which opponent. He had somehow convinced his father – a city councillor – to pull strings to get him in the sportsmen company just to be near his heroes.

"Hard to imagine that I'm just three beds down from Tom Gracie," he gushed. "Did you know he was a reserve for Scotland in 1911, the year they faced England at Goodison Park? That's how he was spotted by Everton and then Liverpool before making the transfer to Hearts..."

And so on, all the way back to the barracks.

"Not a healthy interest," Hugh muttered to Jack that evening as they washed for tea.

Most of the men in the barracks with Jack were well into their twenties, yet the atmosphere was more like a Scout camp with all manner of childish jokes and pranks. One morning Pat Crossan awoke to find he'd been stitched into his bed. But it was inevitable that Ripley would become the favourite victim. He proved a constant annoyance to the footballers with all his questions and helpful statistics.

One evening Crossan was arguing some trivial point with a rival Hibs player and called out to Harry Wattie, "How many goals did you have in home matches last season?"

Wattie replied, "How should I know? Ask Ripley."

And of course Ripley had the answer in an instant – along with total career goals scored both home and away.

"How do you know all this stuff?" Wattie asked, incredulous.

"I just do," said Ripley. "Ask me my mother's birthday and I couldn't tell you."

Jack also soon discovered that it had been Ripley snoring that first night – and every night thereafter. It was a marvel to think anyone so small could make so much noise. He kept all the men awake.

One night Crossan and Wattie had enough. Ripley had fallen into an exhausted sleep and began his usual loud rhythmic snore. There was much whispered recruiting, and eight men took hold of Ripley's bed and carried it down three flights of stairs as he slept. That next morning he awoke shivering and found his bed in the centre of the parade ground. A sentry stood over him along with Regimental Sergeant Major Muir.

"Seems your bed's gone a wandering, soldier," he said.

But of course that didn't stop the snoring.

The only player who spared Ripley grief was Tom Gracie. Certainly he was the most sensible man in the barracks and the one Jack most admired. Age 25 he had come to Hearts on a £400 transfer fee from Liverpool but had grown up in Glasgow. He was a talented and clever footballer – a top scorer – but, unlike most of the other first-team men, modest about his skill.

The first time Gracie shook hands with Jack he said with a wry smile, "McCartney tells me I'd better keep an eye on you if I want to hold onto my job."

"Not a chance," replied Jack.

"Don't undersell yourself," said Gracie. "I've watched you play."

Jack shook his head but thought it just about the best compliment he'd ever been paid.

Christmas approached and hard as Jack found the early training, neither he nor any of the other men suffered any shortage of food or warm bedding. One thing the battalion did lack though was uniforms. Most of the men were still training in the civilian clothes in which they mustered – marching in street shoes, climbing hills in thin wool overcoats. The clothes were growing ragged with hard wear and repeated soakings in the cold rain.

"We'll be down to our pyjamas by the time we get to France," Crossan grumbled.

McCrae and the rest of the officers were all too aware of the problem but there was a nationwide shortage of khaki. Other units had been waiting even longer. It seemed ridiculous that they should be defeated by a simple lack of proper shoes.

Two days before Christmas the entire battalion was invited to attend the pantomime at the King's Theatre – a special performance of *Jack and the Beanstalk*. Parts of the script had been rewritten with references to the war and there was much cheering and shouting. Jack sat with Hugh and Ripley near the back of the theatre and could barely hear the actors saying their lines.

Halfway through the second act there was a scene where the character of Jack, having climbed the beanstalk, raps with his sword on the portals of the giant's castle. The doors swung open revealing Sir George in full uniform. A roar of approval rose from the audience. In his hand the Colonel held a slip of paper from which he read the verse:

> "Do not ask where Hearts are playing and
> look at me askance.
> If it's football that you're wanting you must
> come with us to France."

McCrae then thanked the men for their hard work and promised a special surprise for that next day. During the morning drill two lorries appeared at headquarters. One of the sergeants yelled to the assembled men, "Father Christmas has come early, boys!"

Inside were over 2,000 uniforms and 4,000 pairs of boots. Later a rumour circulated that senior officers under McCrae's leadership had used a crowbar to break into a North British Railway supply depot. Here they stole a consignment of khaki cloth and other gear bound for a unit in the south, from which uniforms had been manufactured in record time.

On 25 December crowds gathered along Princes Street and, to the beat of pipe and drum, McCrae's battalion marched out in their crisp new tunics. This was followed by a traditional turkey dinner in the mess hall.

Later, as Jack tucked into Christmas pudding along with the rest of the sportsmen, he heard Crossan comment to Harry Wattie, "You know this army lark ain't all bad."

10. MAROON AND KHAKI

Hearts played their second match of 1915 on 9 January against Greenock Morton. The entire battalion attended courtesy of the club. Jack and Ripley stood with the rest of the soldiers in the terraces, their breath steaming in the cold air. But it was a disappointing match. Gracie scored the only goal on a header from Scott, even though he had been unwell for most of the week. Next day the newspapers reported that Hearts looked "sluggish" and questioned whether military life was "altogether agreeing" with them.

Certainly the relentless training was taking a toll – endless drill, daily route marches in the cold wet countryside. A few players had to wear oversized football boots to accommodate the dressings on their blisters. Influenza raged among the recruits and often Hearts were forced to play with a reduced squad. But the team was still neck and neck with Celtic in the League Championship and hopes remained high.

The next home match was against Dundee. Hearts were two goals down by half-time but Gracie came through again, scoring from a pass off the winger. Bryden then equalised and Gracie made it three to win with a well-placed free kick.

Jack went down to the changing room after the match to look for the trainer and came upon Gracie sitting slumped on a bench by the lockers. His face was ashen.

"Are you okay?" Jack asked.

Gracie shook his head. "Just feeling a bit weedy."

"Should I get the trainer?"

"No. I'll be okay in a minute or two," he replied.

Jack sat down on the bench next to him. "Are you sure?"

Gracie offered a weak smile. "I'm fine. So how are you holding up with all this training?"

Jack shrugged. "Okay. It beats steering a mail trolley around an office."

Gracie laughed. "Well, I can't argue with that. I started out as a bookkeeper's clerk before signing on with Airdrieonians. My father insisted I have a trade."

"Same as mine," said Jack.

Gracie reached down to untie the laces on his boots.

"Not bad advice. But I could never stick an office job. For me it's always been football – that or nothing."

He then stared a moment at the floor. "Are you ever worried?" he asked.

"Worried about what?" Jack replied.

"Being a soldier; facing the enemy."

"I try not to think about it."

Gracie laughed again but without any joy. "Maybe that's the best thing for it – not to think too much."

Jack did have plenty else on his mind that winter. Hearts second team also struggled with sickness and exhaustion. In addition to army training they were working out three evenings a week with the club and playing matches most Saturdays. Not even Ripley's snoring could keep Jack awake the instant his head touched the pillow.

By the end of February the second team had lost only two of their regular season matches. Jack was lead scorer and more often than not on passes from Hugh Wilson. In one hard-fought match against Hibs, Jack drove in a header off a Wilson pass in the last thirty seconds of play to equalise. Local sports writers began to take notice of Jack Jordan – as did McCartney the manager.

In late March a reserve centre forward on the first team tore a ligament in his knee. That Wednesday the trainer suggested to Jack he check the list for Saturday's match against Clyde. Here he found his name just under Tom Gracie.

His heart beat wildly as he hurried through the gates at Tynecastle and headed up Gorgie Road towards Fountainbridge. Jack figured no one at the barracks would miss him for the five or ten minutes it would take to pop home and announce the news. Letting himself in the front door he met his father in the hall. Tom Jordan smiled but looked sombre. Jack then heard his mother crying in the kitchen.

"What's wrong?" he asked.

Tom shook his head.

"Your mother got a letter from Aunt Rose in Glasgow. The family received a telegram from the War Office. Dougie is missing in action, presumed dead."

Jack was stunned. His cousin Dougie was only two years older and had visited Edinburgh for his holidays every summer Jack could remember. Just out of school he joined the Royal Engineers and had gone to France with the British Expeditionary Force.

"I thought he wasn't even fighting. Just digging trenches," said Jack.

Tom shrugged. "The telegram said it was an artillery barrage."

Jack went into the kitchen and found his mother slumped at the table before a basin of unpeeled potatoes. He sat in the chair next to her and put his arm around her shoulder.

"Promise you'll take care," she sobbed. "Promise."

Tom later saw him to the door but Jack didn't mention the news about his place on the first team. It seemed trivial now.

That Saturday Jack dressed with the rest of the players in maroon and white but there was little of the usual banter. Wattie had lost his father to influenza earlier that month. Gracie had been ill again all week but had risen from his sickbed to play the match.

Jack sat on the bench during the first half, which was goalless. The second half was well advanced before Jamie Low scored. Gracie soon made it two but then lost pace and seemed to have trouble breathing.

McCartney shouted back to the bench, "Jordan! Warm up."

There were ten minutes left of regular play. Jack jogged and jumped in place until McCartney called him to the line.

"Give it your best, lad," he said and signalled a substitution.

Gracie smiled as they passed on his way back to the bench. His face looked deathly pale. Jack took up position, feeling small and exposed in the centre of that vast arena with its roaring crowd.

Play was mostly defensive, the score being two-nil to Hearts. Much of the action now centred around the Hearts goal, as Clyde tried to get something on the board. Then one of the forwards took a shot from far outside the box, which was saved easily by the Hearts goalie. He cleared it with a long low kick. Jack raced under the ball towards the Clyde goal. A defender checked the ball and fumbled about looking for a pass. Here Jack saw his opportunity. He charged in and tapped the ball between the Clyde player's legs. An excited cheer burst from the crowd.

Dribbling forward, Jack looked right and saw Wattie being held back by another defender. To the left was empty pitch. Ahead a lone centre back rushed in for a tackle. Jack raced left and then cut right, wrong-footing the man. Ten yards out he took the shot, which blistered past the goalie's outstretched hands just inside the right post.

The crowd roared its appreciation, though it mattered little to the score. Everyone loves a debut goal. The rest of the match was a blur for Jack and at the final whistle Crossan and Wattie lifted him jokingly onto their shoulders.

Back in the changing room the trainer waited to tell them that Tom Gracie had been taken by cab to the Royal Infirmary.

That next evening after tea, Jack paid Gracie a visit on the respiratory ward of the hospital along with Hugh and Ripley. It was a long airy room with high ceilings and a dozen beds down each wall. Tom was sitting up, reading a newspaper.

"What – no flowers?" he called.

Jack thought he looked ghastly: skin grey, cheeks sunken, eyes hollowed.

Ripley laid a chocolate bar on the bedside table.

"Thanks – you're a lifesaver," said Gracie. "The food here is inedible even by army standards." But he left the chocolate unopened.

"Have the doctors said when you might be getting out?" asked Jack.

"No one's said anything," he replied. "But I've never been more poked and prodded in all my life."

"Maybe some rest will do the trick," said Ripley.

"Maybe," said Gracie, and turned to Jack. "Glad to hear you didn't lose the game for us in the last five minutes – and a goal no less. That was some debut."

"I was lucky," said Jack.

"You have to make your luck," replied Gracie. "So did you enjoy it?"

Jack tried to answer but felt the words catch in his throat.

"I think it was maybe the best moment of my life."

Gracie smiled.

"I still feel a little like that every time I step out onto a pitch."

The sister in charge chased them out of the ward after about half an hour and all three left the grim Victorian building in silence, feeling oddly haunted by the visit.

Gracie did not score again that season, although he still managed to tie with an Ayr United player as top goal scorer of the 1914–15 season. Three weeks later Celtic won the league by only four points with Hearts having drawn one and lost two of their remaining three games. The *Evening News* summed up the feeling in Edinburgh over the dashed expectations of the club:

> Hearts have laboured over these past weeks under a dreadful handicap, the like of which our friends in the west cannot imagine. Between them the two leading Glasgow clubs have not sent a single prominent player to the army. There is only one football champion in Scotland, and its colours are maroon and khaki.

Jack made the bench as substitute in the final matches and saw some play but managed no more goals. He finished his trial uncertain of having done enough to convince McCartney to keep him on for another season. He could only hope – but of course the hopes of any one man are of little account in a world at war.

11. QUIET ENDURANCE

The 16th Royal Scots – the Hearts Battalion – paraded one last time in Edinburgh on 18 June. Jack and over a thousand men assembled on the playgrounds at Heriot's in uniform with full packs. The pipers struck up *Miss Drummond of Perth* and the soldiers marched down the Mound and along Market Street to Waverley Station. Here a vast crowd spilled out onto Princes Street, blocking traffic.

Families and relatives crowded the southbound train platform to see off sons, brothers, fathers. Jack pushed through the throng trying to find his parents and sister. It seemed unreal to think they were finally heading off to war. All around him were men saying their farewells. Jack saw Ripley stiffly shake hands with his father. Annan Ness held his baby girl as his wife clutched at his arm. Pat Crossan stood chatting with Harry Wattie and his parents, holding hands with a pretty girl who turned out to be Harry's little sister Alice. Pat had given her an engagement ring just the week before, to the surprise of everyone. Hugh Wilson had already boarded the train, not wanting to see all the turmoil.

Jack spotted his sister and waved. Behind her stood his mother, clinging for support on the arm of Tom Jordan. This was his small family, his world for the last eighteen years. And now they were to be pulled apart. For the first time Jack felt real panic.

They had only minutes but no one could think what to say. So Jack hugged his mother and sister each in turn and turned to his father.

"I'd better go and find Hugh," he said.

Tom Jordan shook his hand.

"We're as proud of you as we can be," he said, heavily. "Take care now."

Jack dared not look him in the face.

The train took them to Ripon in Yorkshire. On arrival they formed a long column and marched three miles in oppressive heat to an army camp near the ancient ruins of Fountains Abbey. Here they joined two other battalions from Lincolnshire and Glasgow to form the 101st Brigade. They were housed in twelve-man tents, and a lottery was organised among the men to determine who would share with Ripley.

"This is bigotry pure and simple," he complained. "I may snore but have you smelled Crossan's feet?"

Over the weeks to follow Jack took part in "brigade manoeuvres" which involved digging trenches and fighting mock battles with the English soldiers. He learned how to rapid-fire his rifle and thrust a twelve-inch bayonet into a sandbag dressed to resemble an enemy soldier.

"Fine as long as the sandbag isn't trying to stick you back," Hugh had said.

Each morning the sun beat down upon the dusty training ground and some afternoons tremendous thunderstorms would roll in over the hills. One day lightning struck one of the tents, killing a man. But it was the heat and exhaustion that took the greatest toll among the men – including Tom Gracie.

He had never been right again after that winter at Heriot's, and when the weather improved and the battalion left Edinburgh he seemed little better. A slight man anyway, he grew even more scarecrow-like.

One hot afternoon the brigade set off on a fifteen-mile march in full packs. Tom had only gone a couple of miles before he collapsed on the road and had to be taken back to camp on a farmer's cart. Returning that evening Jack learned he'd been admitted to the field hospital.

Jack visited Gracie later after supper. He lay under a wool blanket though the room was stifling. He appeared even more emaciated, if that was possible. Jack sat on the edge of the bed. Gracie smiled.

"Looks like you've got an open shot at centre forward," he said.

"Not a chance," Jack replied. "You'll be up again by tomorrow."

"No. They're sending me to Leeds Infirmary this time," said Gracie. "More poking and prodding."

"Maybe they'll find out what's wrong this time," said Jack.

"Maybe," he replied.

But Gracie evaded the topic and asked about the

latest rumour that the 16th was bound for Egypt. Every day it seemed a different story circulated the camp. Jack shook his head.

"Muir says it's still France."

"Too bad," said Gracie. "I always fancied a ride on a camel. Maybe next war."

Jack stayed the full hour and just before leaving he reached out to shake Gracie's hand. The once firm grip was now weak and bony.

"Keep your head down, Jordan," he said. "Looks like you might ship out before me."

"Don't be daft," Jack replied. "I'll be back to see you tomorrow."

But that next morning an ambulance took Gracie away.

In September the entire brigade moved to Sutton Veny on Salisbury Plain for divisional training – mock assaults on imaginary German trenches, more tactical route marches and weapons practice.

On 23 October Jack played centre forward in the Divisional Football Championship. McCrae's battalion defeated the 18th Northumberland Fusiliers – Jack scoring one of his team's six goals. Just after the match Sir George gathered the players together and announced that Tom Gracie had that morning died of leukaemia at Stobhill Hospital in Glasgow.

Gracie had known of the diagnosis since that March day Jack subbed for him in the Clyde match but had told no one apart from his manager. He'd stuck to his football and army training hoping for the best. On 26 October he was buried at Craigton Cemetery within sight of Ibrox Stadium.

Jack was stunned by the news as were the rest of his team-mates – and even in all the death that was to follow, he never forgot Gracie and his quiet endurance.

Two months later the battalion broke camp again and entrained for Southampton. Here they boarded a paddle-wheel steamer called the *Empress Queen*. It had been a pleasure craft before being converted into a troop carrier and painted a dull grey. The Channel crossing was choppy and Jack stood up on deck most of the journey feeling seasick and nervous of German U-boats.

Hugh joined him as the steamer approached the coast, and the lights of the French port of Le Havre drew nearer. Jack felt as if it were time itself ploughing ahead through the water, bearing him towards some unseen fate. Nothing he could do would stop that progress. Hugh spoke quietly at his side.

"Will you write to my sister Emily if anything happens to me?"

"Nothing's going to happen," said Jack.

"Just in case then."

He gave Jack a slip of paper.

"If you lose it just remember my aunt's married name – Nandi. Not many of those in Durham."

"I won't lose it," said Jack.

Hugh stared across the water to the harbour lamps.

"She'll take it hard – having already lost her ma and all."

Jack nudged him with his shoulder.

"Come on – I wager this time next year we'll both be back scoring goals at Tynecastle."

The ship docked at midnight. Dawn broke over a

bleak winter landscape, fields brown and damp, trees bare of leaves. Smoke rose from the chimneys of the distant town where a train awaited to carry them east towards the rumbling guns of the Front.

12. THE PUSH – JULY 1916

It was just before sunrise. The ground quaked with a massive bombardment – each explosion rattling the gear in Jack's haversack, lighting up the blasted landscape around him. Curtains of dirt, hundreds of feet high, rose over the valley to the east where the German front line was being pounded by British artillery.

"Do you think anything could survive that?" Hugh shouted in Jack's ear.

"Hard to imagine how," he shouted back.

And yet in the last week a captured soldier had told officers that the Germans had a warren of dugouts, some of them forty feet deep in the chalk subsoil and reinforced with concrete, timber supports and steel doors. Just as soon as the shelling stopped, the enemy troops would dig themselves out and reoccupy the trenches.

Seven days now the heavy field guns of the divisional artillery had been "softening" the German defences for the big push scheduled to begin in a few hours time. Each shell flash lit the faces of the fifteen other men in Jack's section of C Company. Most sat pale and unspeaking, especially the older men with wives and children. But some of the younger lads cracked jokes:

"Hey, Jim. I forgot my rifle."

"Never mind, pal. Take mine. I'll bide my time 'til you get back."

Next to them Ripley sat with his head resting against his rifle, fast asleep despite the deafening bombardment. Two weeks ago all the men in the battalion had been told to copy out the "Short Form of Will" on page twelve of their pay books. This instructed the "disposal of any property and effects in event of death". Ripley had flat refused.

"Dying is not in my plans," he had said.

"It's not in anyone's plans, you damn fool," the sergeant major had growled.

But no one could persuade him otherwise, not even Captain Coles. And they had already seen so much death in the last six months. Just a few nights before, a patrol from A Company was caught out in no man's land between the front lines. The Germans put up flares. Four men were cut down by machine-gun fire, including Edward Watt, who was only seventeen.

A week before that Fred Bland and his pal Campbell Munro had just sat down for a cup of tea when the Germans began to shell the support line. Shrapnel burst down the entrance to their dugout and killed Fred instantly. Campbell was almost untouched. Before that it was Willie Brydie from Merchiston dropped by a sniper bullet and Donald MacLean killed in a rifle grenade attack, along with John Miller who was with his brother Tommy, both having enlisted together at Tynecastle during the interval at a Hearts v Hibs match.

More than a dozen men had been killed since the battalion landed in France. Somehow the bare fact of this defied belief. Jack still found himself seeking their faces among the ranks.

That morning the sun rose in a clear blue sky. It would be another hot day. Just before 7.00 the roar of artillery grew even more intense in advance of the main assault. It was said that nearly a quarter of a million shells – 3,500 per minute – fell on the German lines in the final hour of the bombardment. The steady rumble could be heard as far away as Hampstead Heath in London.

The lead batallions readied themselves to go over first. C Company would be in the second wave. It had all been rehearsed two weeks before in a French farm field in the rear of the line. Flags and red ribbon had marked out the six lines of German defences with signposts for the trenches – Heigoland, Bloater, Kipper, Sausage Redoubt. The generals had worked it all out on paper just as the training manuals advised. Jack and the rest of the troops jogged across the muddy field in orderly ranks, overrunning imaginary enemy positions before being returned to camp each evening in trucks.

Now the day had arrived – 1 July 1916. No more rehearsals.

All along a fourteen-mile front north and south of the river Somme the British and French forces would attack, driving the Germans into retreat. It was meant to turn the tide of the war, to break the long stalemate on the Western Front – an unbroken line of trenches and defensive positions that stretched 472 miles from the North Sea coast south to the Swiss border.

McCrae's 16th Battalion and the rest of the 34th Division had the task of capturing German trenches and two fortified villages along a mile front over shell-torn ground strung with thick tangles of barbed wire. The artillery bombardment had been intended to destroy this wire so that British troops could get a clear run on the attack. But after seven days much of the wire still lay in place.

Jack checked his pocket watch again. The minutes seemed endless. Platoon Sergeant Sandy Yule huddled in among the men. In civilian life he was a hose maker at the North British Rubber Company – a giant of a man but with a gentle manner. A ripple of movement drifted down the line as Captain Coles appeared from the dugout smoking his pipe. The final order had been given. Sergeant Yule turned to Jack and the rest of his men.

"Steady lads," he said. "Remember you're Royal Scots. You mind your pals and they'll mind you."

All that remained now was the waiting.

13. THE WHISTLE

Jack Jordan stood in position against the front wall of the trench. Sweat soaked into his shirt and tunic. Gripped across his chest was a short magazine Lee-Enfield rifle with barrel-mounted bayonet, on his head a steel helmet. He had left his full pack and greatcoat behind but carried a haversack containing a mess kit and utensils, gas helmets and extra socks. Among his other equipment were two 3 lb Mills hand grenades and ammunition including two fifty-round bandoleers, along with a water bottle. All together Jack carried around 60 lbs – a fact that can be estimated with fair accuracy.

But there were other burdens and these not so

easily tallied: the choking fear, the certain realisation that forward was the only direction possible; to go back or refuse to go at all meaning dishonour and a firing squad.

At 7.20 Jack felt the ground shudder with a tremendous explosion. A few miles north the earth erupted in a towering geyser of rock and soil. British "sappers" had tunnelled deep under the German lines and planted huge explosive mines. Eight minutes later two more mines exploded almost directly in front of the forward trench; the largest blasted dirt over 4,000 feet into the air. The German soldiers in positions directly above were obliterated.

Two minutes later at 7.30 the whistles blew and Jack shifted into position ready to mount his ladder. Beside him stood Alfie Briggs – a riveter from Partick and star half-back on Hearts first team. They heard the sound of the pipers from the 15th starting up with *Dumbarton's Drums* as the lead ranks emerged from their trenches and set off down the hill.

Hopes that the mines and the bombardment had destroyed the enemy were dashed almost immediately by the frenzied rattle of German machine-guns. Jack could only just imagine the effect of this fire cutting into the men. Dirt and debris rained down on the trench from exploding shells as German field guns targeted the advancing troops. Hugh crouched next to Jack, his face tense and pinched like a boy waiting his turn on the high diving platform.

It was four minutes after the whistle before McCrae's battalion began to advance. A shout rose from the line as men scrambled out of the trenches. Jack grabbed the ladder and clambered up. No man's land opened before him in a haze of smoke and dirt; bullets and shrapnel whistled through the air. He put his head down and broke into a stumbling run under the weight of his gear.

A shell exploded directly ahead and Jack saw two men fall. Big Sandy Yule stopped and slung his rifle, before lifting both soldiers by their belts and carrying them back to the trench. A few seconds later he passed again, racing towards the lead ranks advancing into the acrid smoke.

Dead and wounded soldiers from the first attack littered the ground. Jack tripped over a body and dropped his rifle. He looked down to see it was Tommy Hogg from A Company, blood spreading across his tunic from a chest wound. Beside him lay his best pal Steven Morris, killed instantly in the same burst of shrapnel.

Jack stared aghast until someone behind him growled, "Get a move on, Jordan."

It was Lieutenant Fields with his service revolver drawn. So Jack picked up his rifle and set off again.

A few minutes later he reached the first German line and leapt down into the abandoned trench. Sandy Yule and the rest of the platoon were now clambering up the far side. Jack felt a wild hope. The Germans had fled. He slung his rifle and followed. Reaching the lip he saw the muzzle flash of a German machine-gun to the left and hesitated.

A voice behind snarled, "Move it."

Jack crawled over the edge of the trench on all fours.

Just then Frank Mackie, one of the Mossend players, leapt over him and shouted, "Come on boys. We've got them on the run."

Twenty paces on, a shell exploded at Frank's heels; nothing remained of him when the smoke cleared.

More men dashed past Jack so he picked himself up again.

A cluster of British soldiers was held up before a line of tangled wire. A machine-gun cut into them with terrible effect. Jack watched as Tam Ward rushed the position with a squad of men. The

Germans kept firing right up to the moment they were overrun, and then threw up their hands in surrender. All were shot.

Jack hadn't even time to register the horror. More troops now from D Company swept forward and Jack followed, crossing a second German trench with more open ground beyond. The church tower in the village of Contalmaison now seemed close. This was their objective.

Jack caught sight of his platoon ahead and dashed over the open ground to catch up. Another German machine-gun opened up from a hidden dugout to the left. Jack was ten yards behind when he saw Sandy Yule jerk wildly to the side as a bullet struck his left arm. Another burst shattered both his legs and he dropped heavily to the ground. Briggs fell in the same burst.

Jack froze, and in that moment felt a tremendous blow to his right leg, which swept him off his feet. Rolling onto his side he reached down to his knee and pulled his hand away slick with blood. He tried to stand up but a searing pain ripped through his thigh and he fell back to the ground breathless.

All around him the gunfire grew more intense. Bullets and shrapnel showered the ground like raindrops. He sat up and shouted for help. A second blow struck him hard in the back of the head. Jack's last memory as he tumbled forward was of roaring darkness; all light and air sucked from the world.

14. IN NO MAN'S LAND

It could have been a minute or an hour later that Jack awoke with a tearing agony in his leg. He opened his eyes to see drifting clouds of dust and smoke against a brilliant blue sky. Someone had him under each arm and was dragging him over the rough ground.

Hot metal fizzed in the air. The soldier pulled him into a deep shell crater. Jack looked around. It was Hugh.

"You stay put. I'll be back," he shouted before disappearing over the edge of the crater. That was the last Jack saw of Hugh Wilson that day or ever after.

He drifted back into unconsciousness and awoke later under a fierce sun. His clothes were drenched in sweat, his lips cracked and blistered. He reached up to find his hair caked in dried blood. The slightest movement made both his knee and head throb in unison – two opposite poles of pain. He was also desperately thirsty.

Jack unhitched the water bottle from his belt but found that it had been drained empty. A nick in the canvas sling told where shrapnel had punctured the metal. He looked around in desperation, and that's when he saw the soldier half buried in the slope above. He couldn't see the man's face – just the rise of his back and an arm stretched out towards the lip of the crater. But the uniform appeared to be that of a Royal Scot.

"Can you hear me?" Jack shouted.

But the man didn't move.

Jack turned away and tried to calm the sudden horror he felt; the fear that he too would bleed to death in this dirt hole. He reached down again to his knee, the trousers torn and sticky. With difficulty he managed to pull off his tunic and use it to bind the joint.

All that long morning, artillery shells rained down around him while machine-guns raked the open ground. No one dared move. Fighting was now back in the trenches and Jack was cut off at least until nightfall.

By mid-afternoon he was almost insane with thirst. Nothing else mattered beyond finding water. He pushed himself crab-like up the slope of the crater and, when in reach, grabbed the boot of the dead soldier and pulled. The corpse slid down in an avalanche of dirt.

Jack just barely recognised it as Tom Haldane from the 15th – his face already black-blue and swollen. In civilian life he'd been a butcher on Easter Road with a wife and young kids. Jack found an almost full bottle of water hitched to his belt. He tried to just sip but found himself sucking down the warm liquid in gulps. Almost immediately the throbbing in his head eased. Saving a third of the water he then rolled Haldane back onto his side and covered his face with a ground sheet before pushing himself to the far end of the crater. Here he waited for darkness.

Amidst the shell blasts and bursts of gunfire Jack could hear other wounded soldiers, their groans and pleas for help. One man cried incessantly, "Archie, Archie," until his voice grew weak and stopped altogether.

Jack slipped in and out of consciousness and

awoke sometime later in the night. In the flash of the artillery fire he checked his watch but then remembered it had been smashed during the attack. He rolled over onto his side. Another shell-burst lit the crater and Jack noticed then that the corpse had vanished. In the next flash he looked again but the crater was empty. He felt a sudden choking fear.

Either the body had moved or been moved. But Jack knew Tom was dead; he'd seen the man's face. Then in the moonlight he caught a glint of metal. Keeping his eyes on that point until the next flash he saw three fingers sticking up from the soil, one wearing a gold wedding band. A shell must have struck near the edge of the crater collapsing the side and burying Tom where he lay.

Jack took a sip of water and tried to calm his nerves. Someone would come for him; it was only a matter of waiting. He considered crawling up to the open ground but each time he moved, the wound in his knee sent hot stabs of pain up his thigh. Just before daybreak he lost consciousness and awoke again under a blistering sun.

The snipers and machine-guns were well at work, firing on anything that moved. Jack could taste blood in his mouth from his cracked lips. He drained the last drops from the water bottle and made a low shelter to shade his face using his rifle and tunic. Tonight he'd have to move as there would be no surviving a third day out in the open.

The next twelve hours were the longest of Jack's life. By midday he grew delirious with thirst and began to hallucinate. Hearts manger John McCartney appeared at the edge of the crater in his suit and bowler hat.

"Come on. Up you get, son," he barked.

"But I'm shot," Jack argued.

"Nonsense," he replied. "It's just a sprain."

Later it was Gracie crouched at the far edge of the crater, no more than a skeleton in pyjamas. He stared at Jack out of hollow black eyes but said nothing. All day he vanished and reappeared as though waiting for an end.

Night fell and Jack began to feel a little more himself in the cooler air. He managed to rebind his knee and brace it tightly with a bayonet. He then took a breath and began to crawl. Just a few yards at a time, up and over the steep edge of the crater. Even that small distance left him exhausted from the pain. A quarter-moon lit the torn landscape. He took a rough bearing on the hills and began to move in what he figured was the direction of the British lines.

Jack had gone only about thirty yards when a figure emerged from the darkness, moving towards him fast and low. There was no way of knowing if the Germans had reoccupied the line and this was now an enemy soldier. He fell back and lay motionless but soon found a bayonet pointing in his face. Death had finally come.

But the soldier peered down and whispered, "Is that you, Jack?"

Standing there above him, moonlight glinting off his spectacles, was Albert Ripley. Jack was unable to answer; he could only turn away and weep.

Ripley left him with a full water bottle and ran to find help. Soon two men appeared with a stretcher and carried him to the forward command post. Here Colonel McCrae and a handful of Royal Scots fought off counterattacks in the confused warren of enemy trenches and redoubts. Jack and the rest of the wounded spent the next 24 hours in a German bunker thirty feet below ground. It had been untouched by the shelling and was wired with electricity.

A day later the battalion was relieved from the line by troops from the 23rd Division. Jack was carried to a rear casualty clearing station before being taken to a makeshift hospital in a small village primary school. Drawings made by the long evacuated children hung on the wall opposite his bed – houses with curls of smoke from the chimneys, bright green gardens, stick-figure families.

The nurses gave him laudanum, which dulled the pain but brought on vivid nightmares where soldiers that he knew were dead crowded around his bed like moths drawn to a flame.

Over 800 men from the four companies of the 16th Royal Scots – the Hearts Battalion – had taken part in the assault on 1 July 1916. Three days later when the ragged battalion assembled again for roll call at Long Valley near Millencourt nearly 640 men did not answer when their name was called. In that single day fighting at the Somme over 19,000 British soldiers died and another 35,000 were wounded.

Jack's head wound had not been serious. The bullet only grazed his skull. But the surgeon warned early on that he might lose his right leg. A bullet had entered the side of his knee and shattered the joint. In the long delay reaching hospital, infection had set in and for weeks the wound refused to heal – leaking a thin, watery pus into the cotton dressing.

But within a few weeks the nurses had Jack up on crutches and the skin slowly closed over, although the joint remained stiff and immovable. No one had to tell Jack that his football career was over.

Three months later Jack returned to Edinburgh with a medical discharge. The North British Rubber Company took him back in a promoted position as assistant clerk. Most nights he awoke crying in his sleep, his bedclothes damp and tangled. Try as he might to banish the horrors from his waking memory they always returned in his dreams.

One sunny afternoon that October, Jack's older sister Mary took him for a stroll in Princes Street Gardens. She left him sitting on a bench in front of the Castle Fountains as she went for ice creams. Two girls of thirteen or fourteen sat on a bench opposite stealing shy glances in his direction. Jack's crutches were tucked out of sight behind the bench and he was no longer in uniform.

The bolder of the two girls rose from the bench as the other covered her face and giggled. She was a pretty girl with blue eyes and long strawberry-blonde hair curling over the shoulders of her Sunday dress. Over she came and stood before Jack with a haughty tilt of chin.

Jack glanced up and smiled. From her pocket she drew a single white feather and held it out before him on the palm of her hand.

15. NOT FORGOTTEN

The clock stands in a traffic island at the busy junction outside Haymarket railway station. It has a double-sided face and is set within a large stone memorial, weathered and blackened with exhaust fumes. Each day commuters stream by on their way to and from their trains. To most it's all but invisible amid the surrounding buildings, the signs and traffic lights, the rush of cars and buses. Bolted into the stone on one side of the monument is a bronze plaque that reads:

ERECTED BY
THE HEART OF MIDLOTHIAN
FOOTBALL CLUB
TO THE MEMORY OF
THEIR PLAYERS AND MEMBERS
WHO FELL IN THE GREAT WAR
1914–1919

Ross must have ridden past it dozens of times in the car without taking any notice. The afternoon he and Pat walked down to Haymarket they found the stone scrawled with spray paint. Scour marks showed where the council regularly cleaned off the graffiti.

Pat had brought along an old pamphlet that said the monument had been erected in 1922, four years after the war ended. An estimated 40,000 people had crowded into Haymarket on the day it was dedicated, along with pipe bands and ministers and politicians. Sir George McCrae himself had been present on the platform along with some of the few remaining survivors of the original Hearts Battalion.

Big Sandy Yule was there, having recovered from his wounds, as was Alfie Briggs who, like Jack, would never play football again. Among other former Hearts players present were Annan Ness and Jamie Low as well as Pat Crossan, who did make the return to Tynecastle. The "handsomest man in the world" started again as winger in the first home match of the 1919 peacetime season, defeating Queens Park. A few years later he would marry Alice Wattie after what he called "the longest engagement in Scottish history". Alice's brother and Pat's best pal would not make the ceremony. Harry Wattie died on the first day's fighting at the Somme.

Also present at the ceremony was Albert Ripley, who managed to survive the war despite being wounded twice and later gassed at Roeux. He and Jack Jordan remained lifelong friends. And, of course, Jack was there too among the crowd. By then he'd already met Ross's great-grandmother and they were engaged. A year later Sir George would help him get a position at the Royal Bank of Scotland where he worked until his retirement in 1958, having risen to the position of senior manager.

Over the years Jack rarely spoke of the war and his fallen friends – though he did write each and every Christmas to Hugh Wilson's sister Emily. What Pat knew of her father's story had come from books and what her mother had told her the year after Jack died from cancer in 1960.

For weeks the story of Jack Jordan and the 16th Royal Scots haunted Ross. To think of the immediate world around him – streets, houses, tenements – overlain with time like one of those kid's books with clear plastic pages. Lives all but vanished: hopes, dreams, sorrow, pain.

One night he lay awake in bed thinking about something Pat said. Ross had asked her why people build monuments.

"Isn't it better just to forget?" he said.

"We can't ever forget," she'd replied.

"Why not?"

Pat had stood there by the clock clutching the yellowed pamphlet.

"Well, the way I look at it is – the dead can only be dead. Nothing else is left to them. The least we can do is to try and make sense of what's happened in the past, hold on to what it meant to those soldiers and their families – even if just by reading a name on a bronze plaque."

It was this that gave Ross the idea. The very next evening he phoned Pat and they talked it over. She wrote the letter and in the end it was an archivist from Heart of Midlothian FC who got back in touch.

One day a few weeks later Pat met Ross after school and they took a cab to Tynecastle. The archivist – a Mr Kemp – met them in reception at the club administration building and took them into a meeting room. He was a small portly man, a good six inches shorter than Pat, with balding hair and thick black glasses. Ross laid Jack's box onto the table.

"May I?" said Mr Kemp.

Ross nodded and the archivist reached for the latch. His eyes widened when he opened the lid. He lifted the boots carefully out of the box.

"These have been well looked after. Top quality for the time."

Mr Kemp grew more excited when he found the

maroon jersey, and the shorts and socks – a full kit. But it was the medal and Jack's photograph that he looked at the longest before removing his glasses.

"And you say he never played football again."

"No. Just a loyal supporter after the war," Pat replied.

Mr Kemp shook his head.

"Well, all I can say is the club would be honoured to have these objects in our collection – especially with the upcoming centennial of the Great War."

In the cab on the way home Ross began to wonder if he'd made a mistake giving up Jack's things. Pat seemed almost to read his thoughts. She laid a hand on his knee.

"Why not stop in for a quick cup of hot chocolate and then I'll walk you home."

Sitting later at her kitchen table Ross sighed.

"Do you think it's possible to miss someone you never knew?"

Pat smiled.

"But you do know Jack – or all that's left to know.

And he knew you."

"How could he know me?" asked Ross.

Pat replied, "Well, it's obvious he cherished the items in that box. Why else would he have packed them away so carefully? And he must have trusted that someone would come along who'd recognise their worth."

Ross looked confused. She reached out and touched his hand.

"That was you. And I know for certain that he would have been proud to see his old kit on display at Tynecastle. To remind people just what was sacrificed by all those young men. You made that happen."

Ross felt better about his decision after that. And for the next few weeks he went to bed each night hoping to see Jack again in his dreams, to play once more with him at Tynecastle, to score that perfect goal. But dreams are rarely a matter of will. Nor does true life play out like tales in books. Brave soldiers don't prevail, they mostly suffer or die for no good reason, bad luck or an undone shoelace or some lines on a map.

A few good things did happen in the coming weeks. Somehow Ross managed to "find his feet" as Pat had predicted and no longer tripped over thin air. Indeed, the whole team seemed to up their game towards the end of the season and began to win a few matches. By June, Bruntsfield was progressing up the league. All the whispering about Barry ended and more parents began to turn up for matches. Even Pat appeared at the pitch one Saturday afternoon.

It was a quarter-final match against Clermiston. The Bruntsfield team was down by two goals near the end of the first half. But in the final minute Calum Mitchell managed to score a header. Barry gathered the team together at half-time.

"Tough defending out there and passing looks good, but you forwards need to take some digs. You've got nothing to lose – remember we're just happy to be here."

Going back out onto the pitch Ross noticed a group of S1s had come along to watch, including Craig Muir. He stood near the far goal with his arms folded, looking as large and menacing as ever. Ross had said nothing to his parents about the punch and he hoped Muir appreciated the trouble he'd been saved.

The second-half whistle blew and Ross forgot Muir and everything else in the sudden rush of play. Bruntsfield threatened over a dozen times in the next twenty minutes but just couldn't put the ball in the net. Only five minutes remained in the match when Calum sent a cross from the right wing, which the Clermiston goalie just managed to deflect over the crossbar. It was a corner. Calum lined up for the kick but couldn't see an opening so he motioned Ross back.

With a bit of jostling Ross managed to elude his defender. He took the pass off his right heel and with a quick touch set himself up for the shot. The ball rocketed off his foot, bending between two defenders and past the outstretched gloves of the keeper. It glanced off the far post and into the net – the sweetest shot Ross had ever kicked. A roar went up from the pitch. Even loud-mouth Bob Nelson looked stunned.

The final whistle blew and the game ended at two-all with a penalty shoot-out. Ying looked white-faced and grim.

"I think I might vomit," he said.

Barry pulled him aside.

"Remember, a penalty shoot-out is no-lose situation for a goalie," he said. "All the pressure is on the shooters."

But Ying looked no more reassured.

Bruntsfield won the toss and Ross was first up to shoot. He made it in with an easy chip. After five more shots, the score was three-all. Calum Mitchell lined up for his turn but scooped the ball high over the crossbar. All the Clermiston players mobbed their goalie as though the match was already won.

Ying lined up for the next shot, looking pale but surprisingly determined – waving his arms to distract the Clermiston player. The shooter faked left but was slow in changing direction. Ying read it perfectly and easily deflected the ball.

On the next shot Rory Burn made it five-four to Bruntsfield. The pressure was again on Ying.

The next Clermiston shooter came forward – a large red-haired boy who took so long positioning the ball the referee had to hurry him up. The player then took one step and drilled the shot hard but straight. It hit Ying square in the middle and he looked down in disbelief to find the ball tucked in his arms.

A wild cheer erupted from the sidelines and Ross and the rest of the team rushed forward and hoisted

Ying onto their shoulders. Over on the far end the S1 boys punched the air in triumph. Ross caught sight of Muir who gave him a sly thumbs-up, and it was good to see the guy could forget he was a creep, even if just for a moment.

The Bruntsfield P7s would later be knocked out in the semi-finals but that day they were winners. Barry invited all the players and parents back to his house for a barbeque. He set up an old stereo turntable in the garden and played scratchy jazz records. They ate sausages and hamburgers and later, much to the players' horror, a few of the parents even felt inspired to dance.

In the evening when Pat walked Ross home again she put an arm around his shoulder.

"That was some goal," she said. "You should listen more to your granny."

Another good thing happened a few days later. A letter awaited Ross one afternoon when he arrived home from school. On the envelope was the official Hearts crest. Ross tore it open and inside were two tickets to the season opener – Hearts v Dundee United. There was also a compliments slip with a mysterious note from Mr Kemp: "Look out for a surprise."

The Saturday arrived and Ross of course invited Pat to go with him to the match. The seats were possibly the best in the stadium – midfield, halfway up the stand. They sat down and got settled just as the Hearts players ran out onto the pitch for their warm-up.

Ross was studying his programme when he heard Pat exclaim, "Oh my word!"

He looked up to see her staring in astonishment, and followed her gaze across the pitch. Among the huge posters of famous past Hearts players that decorated the far stand – Tommy Walker, John Cumming, Drew Busby, Steven Pressley – was a new one. Twenty feet high, arms folded and beaming with that same confident grin, stood Jack Jordan, towering over the crowd, eighteen years old and forever fresh with promise.

ACKNOWLEDGEMENTS

Ross, Jack Jordan, his family and some of the characters in this book – including Hugh Wilson and Albert Ripley – are fictional, but the story of the 16th Royal Scots "Hearts Battalion" is a true one. The events are based on real accounts though some particular details have been altered and invented for reasons of plot. But I have attempted to remain true to the story and the period.

This book owes much to the excellent history of the "Hearts Battalion" by Jack Alexander: *McCrae's Battalion: The Story of the 16th Royal Scots* (Mainstream Publishing, 2004). It is a fascinating and painstakingly researched though readable book packed with detail and I thoroughly recommend it to anyone interested in the history of the 16th Royal Scots and World War I.

I would like to thank David Speed, club historian at the Heart of Midlothian, and Craig Murray of the Imperial War Museum who both made comments on the manuscript, though any deviations from historical fact – intentional or not – are entirely my own. I would also like to thank Jim Wilson for his help with football terminology and Alan "Let's make some noise" Duffy for his generous introduction to Tynecastle.

Thanks also to my editor at Floris Books, Sally Polson, and my wife Ann – both of whom made many helpful suggestions on the manuscript.

Finally, I would like to acknowledge the 2008 Bruntsfield P7 girls football team – players and parents – who gave an untutored American an insight into the game and many hours of excitement and enjoyment.

AUTHOR INTERVIEW

Q: Have you always wanted to be an author?

JK [James Killgore]: Maybe not always but I certainly loved books from an early age. One of my favourite memories is when my grandmother used to visit our house and come to my bedroom in the early morning with a cup of sweet milk coffee and a thick book of old fairy tales with amazing illustrations.

Q: When did you start writing?

JK: I started writing short fiction in college – but I was always inventing stories as a kid just like anyone. That's the spark and inspiration in writing and is obviously very important. Beyond that it's developing the craft and that's what I learned more about and practised as I got older.

Q: What inspired you to write Soldier's Game*?*

JK: It started out as a whimsical story that I made up for

my footballing daughter. A young boy sneaks into his granny's attic and finds a pair of boots that belonged to his great-grandfather who was a professional footballer. He wears them one day to a match and finds he's magically transformed into a champion striker.

That might have made a good story on it's own but around the same time I picked up a book called *McCrae's Battalion* by a historian called Jack Alexander. It was about a battalion of soldiers from Edinburgh who fought in World War I at the Battle of the Somme in France. Many were fans and players from the Heart of Midlothian football club and a fair number never returned. It was devastating. After that the two stories sort of merged in my head and the magical element just melted away against the grim truth of what happened to those soldiers.

Q: Why do you think that the story of the Hearts Battalion is important?

JK: I think it's a very personal story. It's easy to get caught up in tactics and statistics and weapons when studying major historical events like WWI. True stories like those from the Hearts Battalion bring home the sad consequences of war – right to our doorsteps. Sometimes as I walk across the Union Canal I imagine those young footballers – Harry Wattie, Jimmy Speedie, Pat Crossan – treading the same pavements, feeling the sun on their faces, unaware of what's coming.

Q: Did you have to do a lot of research to write Soldier's Game?
JK: I did quite a bit of digging but Jack Alexander's book is a very detailed history of the 16th Royal Scots and I owe that book a great deal.

Q: How long did it take you to write Soldier's Game*?*
JK: It's hard to say. I wrote the first draft quite a long time ago – probably over a period of a few months. But I have re-written parts of it and revised the text many times.

Q: Was it difficult mixing history and imagination in your book?
JK: Not as difficult probably as working straight from imagination. The great thing about writing historical novels is that much of the drama is ready made. You only have to bring it alive through characters – real and imagined.

Q: Did you have to change any of the historical facts to make sure that Soldier's Game *was a good story?*
JK: I invented quite a few characters to tell the story but I tried hard not to change anything fundamental –

just small facts. All of history is made up of countless small stories and most of those go unrecorded; that's what makes personal diaries so valuable to researchers. Historical fiction allows you to imagine some of those missing stories.

Q: How did you make the book so realistic?

JK: Just by reading accounts of what happened in history books and then trying to imagine small details. I always remind myself that it's important to make sure you slow things down at points in a story – let your characters live in the moment.

Q: What is your favourite time period?

JK: I grew up near the city of New Orleans in the USA and the American Civil War has always fascinated me. Some of my ancestors fought for the Confederates and the war never seemed that remote even though I was born 94 years after it ended. I also find World War I fascinating and incredibly sad – all those young men marching off to France with such confidence and little idea of what was waiting for them.

Q: Which book would you advise all children to read before they grow up?

JK: I think Roald Dahl is just the best. I had not read any of his books until I was a father and I think I enjoyed reading *Charlie and the Chocolate Factory* and *George's Marvellous Medicine* as much as my kids did listening.

Q: Do you play football?

JK: Where I grew up the sport was American football – though now soccer is huge among kids in the States. I have kicked a ball about with friends but I don't think anybody would call it real football! I do enjoy watching though.

Q: What's the best thing about being an author?

JK: I suppose for me it's a kind of grown-up version of make believe. You only get to live one life but in being a writer you spend a lot of time inventing and inhabiting other lives. I also like to read and research history and when you have a project like a book it gives direction to that. You feel you have a stake in it. In a sense you become part of the history just in writing about it.

DID YOU KNOW?

WORLD WAR I

- The Great War – or World War I as it came to be known – began in August 1914 when Germany invaded France and Belgium, drawing Britain into the Europe-wide conflict.
- Over 65 million soldiers fought in the war, an estimated 21 million men were injured and 8.5 million died, significantly more than the entire population of Scotland today.
- Officers were killed in greater proportions than regular soldiers as they carried revolvers rather than rifles and were easy to spot by the enemy.
- The youngest casualty of WW1 is thought to be Private John Condon of the 2nd Royal Irish Regiment who was just fourteen when he was reported missing, presumed dead on 24 May 1915.

- Much of the conflict was fought in a bloody stalemate along a twisting 472-mile line known as the Western Front, which stretched from the English Channel to the Swiss frontier.
- Among the major battles fought along the Western Front was that of the Somme, which began on 1 July 1916 and lasted until that November.
- America entered the war in 1917, which helped to break the stalemate in favour of the Allies. The war came to an end at 11 am on the 11th day of the 11th month in 1918.
- The Great War was also known in later years as the War to End All Wars. Sadly this would not be the case when, just 21 years later, the Nazi leader Adolf Hitler sent German forces into Poland, sparking World War II.
- Among new weapons introduced or used widely for the first time in World War I were the machine-gun, the tank, poison gas, U-boats, and aeroplanes and Zeppelins for aerial bombardment.
- On 2 April 1916, two German Zeppelins sailed across the North Sea and dropped bombs on Leith and central Edinburgh, causing several deaths, with one bomb hitting the Castle rock.

- Hundreds of memorials were commissioned across Britain to commemorate the men who died in The Great War, from simple plaques in churches, to stone monuments such as the Hearts Memorial, to the grand Cenotaph in London.
- Fields of red Flanders poppies grew along the Western Front after the war, inspiring the British Legion to sell paper poppies to raise funds for wounded soldiers, as it still does today.
- More than a million British women went to work in munitions factories during WWI. Emboldened by this contribution to the war effort, they demanded and won limited voting rights in 1918, with full rights granted in 1928 for all adults over 21.

THE BATTLE OF THE SOMME

- On the first day of battle at the Somme the British army suffered its worst one-day combat loss in history with 19,240 soldiers dead, 35,493 wounded and 2,152 missing.

- The Somme was also the first time the tank was used in battle.
- British "sappers" – many of them miners back home – dug deep tunnels under the German lines to plant huge explosive mines. Sometimes in digging they broke through into enemy tunnels and had to engage German sappers in hand-to-hand combat underground.
- By the end of the Somme offensive, British and French troops had penetrated no more than six miles into occupied German territory.
- On 7 October 1916, a German soldier from the 6th Bavarian Reserves was wounded at the Somme. His name was Adolf Hitler.

HEART OF MIDLOTHIAN FC

- Heart of Midlothian football club was founded in Edinburgh around 1874 and first played in East Meadows Park, with players changing in the upstairs room of a local tavern.

- The club began wearing its characteristic maroon in 1877 and moved to the present site of Tynecastle stadium in 1886.
- Under the leadership of manager John McCartney, Hearts fielded one the best squads in the club's history in 1914 when war broke out.
- Military training took its toil and, though heavily favoured to be League Champions, the club lost out to Celtic by only four points in the 1914–15 season.
- Three Hearts players and uncounted fans lost their lives in that first day of fighting at the Somme, including Harry Wattie, Ernie Ellis and Duncan Currie.
- In 1922 supporters and friends of Heart of Midlothian erected a memorial to the singular sacrifice of the football club in the First World War. In 2009 the clock tower was temporarily moved from its place at Haymarket junction and put into storage to make way for the Edinburgh tram works.